D0990962

THE
HUNTING HOUR

THE HUNTING HOUR

A Novel

FRANK CORSARO AND ANDREW CORSARO

authorHOUSE®

AuthorHouse™
1663 Liberty Drive
Bloomington, IN 47403
www.authorhouse.com
Phone: 1-800-839-8640

Published by AuthorHouse   03/22/2012

ISBN: 978-1-4685-0893-2 (sc)
ISBN: 978-1-4685-0895-6 (hc)
ISBN: 978-1-4685-0894-9 (e)

Library of Congress Control Number: 2011961757

*For all the lawmen
who have worked and died in the gray areas
of police work.*

There is no hunting like the hunting of man, and those who have hunted armed men long enough and liked it, never care for anything else thereafter.

~Ernest Hemingway

THE KILLING

Chapter One

. . . .

This is the way I think it happened. I know these killers. There's an art to it, and, as I see it, this one was an immaculate kill.

He got to the place around dusk and parked his car three cross streets away. His target had been pointed out to him, and he had a full face photo. Thinking of how it would go, he felt a spasm and tightness in his chest. Sometimes they get them when realizing they're bringing down a full grown man that could fight back.

He'd been careful to eat something before the hunt. The stomach can growl on empty and give you away. Next morning, all they found was the suspect's bloody clothes stuffed down a storm drain and a few blood-soaked shoe impressions on the sidewalk.

While waiting for it to happen, he'd probably exhausted his "what ifs". No matter how long you've been at it, you can't escape nerves of some kind. Nerves of anticipation are usually worse than the act itself. Besides—The victim was going to be a cop.

He was due home from a local Baltimore bar called Hogan's Alley, a hole in the wall place known to be a hangout for lawmen.

Dusk thickened into night. Heavy sky. No stars or moon to light the way to a silent death. Victims dispatched this way hardly have time to make a sound; they're usually dead before they even know it. The assassin listened to the buzz of I-95 traffic on the freeway above. The victim would be driving back; Hogan's was too far to walk from. He was known as a heavy drinker and might be showing it, or high on dope, or both! Still his experience on the street counted. He'd acquired a don't give a shit swagger from all those years protected by a badge. This might make it difficult for a straight hit. The assassin had been warned that the cop could be dangerous. The job could turn messy and if he were to fail nailing him, there could be consequences; there are always consequences. His legs suddenly felt cold and cramped.

The only light was a small yellow bulb over the dumpster close to the back entrance to the building where the cop lived. Dressed in black, the assassin eased into the shadows outside the radius of the yellow glow. After parking his car, the target would have to pass him.

And he waited.

For safety's sake, he reached into his hoodie pocket and pulled out a six-inch fixed blade knife from a small leather sheath and bladed the dull side against his wrist to protect the blade. He was sweating. He commanded himself to stop sweating, but his command had come too late. The body has its own ways in survival mode.

He heard the sound of a car coming down the side street, the wheels squeaking as the brakes made its final stop at the house.

He was posed at the periphery of the street's shadows near the dumpster. A trickle of sweat fell off his forehead onto his cheek and hung there.

He heard the muffled "thwak" of the car door being open and shut. A quick look out of the shadow confirmed it could be him.

The sound of the cop's quick approach breathed heavily into the dank night air. Then came a rough cough and the rasp of him spitting twice into the street. He came towards him, defenses down, totally unaware of the danger that waited.

In one silent move, the sweating assassin lunged out of his hiding place and sank the blade deep, deep into the socket between the man's collar bone and neck.

He pulled the blade out in a twisting motion. An eruption of blood shot up into the air. Then another! And another!

As the victim struggled to figure out what the hell was happening to him, he tried grabbing the killer's arm, but the slickness of his own blood made it impossible.

The attacker pushed the bleeding man onto his stomach, his neck now pulsing out volumes of blood.

He thrust the knife handle deep into the man's lower back and felt the spine separating like a tight rope being cut. The man's legs went limp. His head dropped, and his breath went shallow. The killer reached his left hand around the man's forehead and pulled his head off the ground to let him look at the dark sky.

Then he cut his victim's throat.

The assassin listened to the rhythmic suck of the blood and air rushing to escape his victim's gaping wound, allowing death to enter. Sheathing the knife, he almost cut his own hand. He leaned over again and watched his sweat mingling with the blood.

He quickly wiped his face with his sleeve, turned the body over to see if it matched his photo then was momentarily shocked to see how quickly the man's features had taken on a look of peace. He instinctively took the man's wallet and his wrist watch and made his way back to his car. He realized he was now covered in blood so he took off his hoodie, wiped his knife down with it and stuffed it down a storm drain to be lost in the rest of the city's filth.

Only after getting into his car did he look at the wallet. $20.00 and two driver's licenses: Frank Dixon on one, Frank Keaton on the other, the assassin must have wondered which one his victim really was.

Chapter Two

"I still think you should have called me, Marie."

"I thought of it, of course, but I decided not to," and she moved away from me.

"Why?," I asked her back.

"Give me a minute, will you, Johnny? It's been a very rough day," and she reached for the coffee cups. It was past midnight, and we were back in our apartment, Marie was still dressed in her scrubs from work, I in my uniform.

She took off her shoes and planted herself on the couch. She had deliberately stopped fussing in the kitchen to pull herself together. I removed my jacket and sat next to her.

"Frank's body had already been examined and put into the morgue; Duke had just finished his report and told me about finding him." Marie's face tightened, emphasizing the beauty of her high cheekbones. "I was there when the coroner arrived with the body. Ordinarily, Frank's body would have been in the freezer at the Medical Examiner's office, but the Medical Examiner's freezer was already full of bodies. And the overflow storage was at Shock Trauma, only a few blocks away."

"Jesus," I said and shut my eyes against the imagined scene. "Dude," she continued, "August heat can start body decomposition pretty fast, so the coroner worked all night like a beaver. Meanwhile, guess what?"

I didn't guess.

"Another homicide arrived to replace Frank on the slab. The morgue tech was on break, so the coroner had to wait. Last night, it was a war zone in Baltimore—blood all over the streets, ready to be hosed off, before business as usual this morning." Marie sat up and sighed. "When the coroner was done with the autopsy, I went along with Frank and the undertaker to the funeral parlor, then took a cab back home."

"Was Frank . . . ?" I couldn't finish my sentence.

"I—I didn't look—till after he was done. Just like I couldn't call you."

I hung my head.

"I knew you were exhausted from your own nightshift and needed all the good sleep you could get. Besides, you don't call somebody."

"I'm not just 'somebody', Marie," I said testily, raising my head.

"I'm sorry" she said, "You're right. That sounded all wrong. But you don't call someone you love and tell him the man he loved like a brother was laying on a morgue slab at the hospital." Marie looked at me with fatigue clouding her face, and a gentle wrinkle of a smile broke through. She put her cup down and hunkered down next to me on the couch. She kissed me on the forehead—my most vulnerable spot. She quickly slipped into my lap and leaned against me.

"Don't let me fall asleep," she whispered in my ear. I could see how hard she was fighting against the fatigue itching to clobber her. Her eyes closed and in the silence, I realized what a good team we made. Marie Ricaud and myself, John Larkin, both in the service of Baltimore City. We understood what the other saw day in and day out in the city. We were both small town people. I matched her in size and slimness and she said I had a gentle anglo face. Suddenly, she sat up.

"I didn't make it strong enough." She dumped the remains in her cup, then grabbed out of the cupboard two massive ceramic bowls we both loved.

"How did you hear about it?," she asked.

"I, I was asleep at the wheel when it happened. I woke up only when J.B. called—telling me to come down to headquarters. He said it was an emergency but wouldn't say what it was."

"When I got there, I was told to prepare something to say at the service. I was too numb to say or do anything coherent. I kept thinking it was just a bad dream and then I came home—and waited till you got here. And Marie—they're asking for contributions to help with the funeral arrangements—oh, God!"

"Johnny, please, don't blame yourself. You would have done anything to prevent it . . ." And she reached up and grabbed my face between her palms.

"Sometimes, when I look at you, I see Frank, and when I looked down at him laying on that cold slab, I lost my grip. I thought I was seeing you. I look at you now and see you'll always have him with you—and to tell the truth, I don't think I want another cup . . ."

"Tell me one thing, Marie. When the Medical Examiner finished with Frank, was his Marine Corps service ring still on his finger?"

"You know—I noticed it when he first came in. It was where it always was on the ring finger on his left hand."

I just nodded. And there were no more blues to bother with—only a night of comfort in each other's arms.

Chapter Three

. . . .

I suddenly sat up. I wasn't still in my car. I checked my watch. It read 5:04am. Frank had been dead for two days. Marie was still asleep, with her back to me. The early morning light both reflected and etched out her nakedness. I almost reached out to touch its loveliness, but I quietly slipped out of bed and tip-toed into the living room. It was still cool, but the early August heat was beginning to filter into the apartment. My nakedness took some pleasure in that. At 9:30, I'd switch the air conditioner back on to home-saver mode. Marie and I had become cost conscious.

I was sitting on the couch holding a large framed photo of the three of us at the beach. Frank and I in swim trunks, Marie in the middle wearing a white beach robe covering her teal blue bikini. We're standing, posing, with Marie's arms around our shoulders. This was the third time Frank had been with us. Marie and I had met only four months before—at the University of Maryland shock trauma hospital—in the midst of another Baltimore bloodbath. I was there filling out a report on a near fatal shooting. Vital personal information passed between us, before the next emergency wheeled her away. The original beach photo, taken by an obliging passerby, so charmed Marie, that she popped up with a proposal.

"I think this might make a really special Christmas card to send out. Aren't you both tired of all that tinsel crap? We'll sign it the three musketeers under our names."

"No snowman with a carrot nose? Great!" I concurred.

"My sister, Bea, won't like that," Frank objected. "She loves tinsel crap. But except for Bea, I don't send out cards."

"Not even to your parents?" Marie asked wistfully.

"Oh, they've been gone for a long while," Frank mumbled and planted his empty Budweiser can in the sand.

"I'm sorry," Marie said and looked at me.

"You don't have to be," Frank answered. "I think they were better off, gone." He said this with a sad smile on his face, and his hand went through his dark blond hair. I jumped in. "My parents will definitely appreciate this view of their errant boy. They haven't seen me like this since prep school. They have a drawer full of me in uniforms."

"Can I have one more Bud, Miss Marie?" We all chuckled at the Miss, as she obliged.

"Well, when I go home for Christmas," Marie said, handing me one more beer, "I'm going to take a 12 by 9 framed copy of the picture with me. Alicia will just love it."

"Who's Alicia?," Frank asked, cracking open his beer.

"Alicia's my mother," Marie replied.

"You call your mother by her first name?" Frank seemed astonished by the idea.

"Well, she's not my real mother—I mean . . ." And Marie looked at me again. I prompted, so she went on.

"I meant Alicia is not my birth mother—I was adopted when I was two months old."

"I see," said Frank gently. "And what do you call your father?"

"Er—Dad or—Father"

"Why's that?," Frank asked. "Doesn't he deserve some equally intimate cognition?"

"My father died when I was seven years old. I didn't really get to know him—but that's how I became a nurse." And she finished her Coke.

"Well," I offered, "My parents are still there for me. I love them, but I don't really know them. Although I know about them, you understand? It happens. Maybe, someday? Meanwhile we all do the best we can."

"I guess this puts us all in some—well—dysfunctional category—wouldn't you say?," Frank asked.

"I haven't thought of it that way—but I guess—yes," I conceded.

"What do you think, Miss Marie?"

"I think it's time for lunch. Chicken sandwich anyone?" She lifted the top to the cooler and handed them out on little paper plates.

"Well, this only goes to prove what I said." We looked at Frank, waiting for the rest of his thought.

"Just think of this chicken here—all chickens,"

"They grow up—if they grow up—into chicken slices, chicken fingers, chicken nuggets. This little chicken," he said as he raised his sandwich, "was probably a baby chicken, a pullet. The world is beginning to love everything little—baby spinach, baby salad, baby this, baby that," and he paused.

"But what's your point?" Marie sounded exasperated.

"The point is, Miss Marie, this chick proves the prevalence of the dysfunctional in our world."

Now Marie was smiling in confusion.

"These days, none of them—animal, vegetable and even probably mineral has been given a chance to really know their mommies and daddies before," and he munched on his sandwich.

"The price of civilization," Frank concluded.

"What an absolutely antic theory," Marie said.

We had come a long way, Frank and I, from standing in line, polished and creased in our formal dress uniforms, me with my parents in tow, Frank right behind us . . . the loner who had just me, or about to have me as the biggest asshole buddy he's ever had.

It was another August, seven years ago, equally hot, but who cared? We were at the Baltimore Police Academy graduation ceremony, inching toward Al Gore, the principal speaker honoring us newly-sworn officers of his political project funding our training. We, the cream of the crop from criminal justice institutions all over our country, the future breed of officer that was supposed to think outside the box and permanently heal Baltimore's dying neighborhoods.

"You should be proud of yourselves," Gore said, and meaning it while craning his neck to read our name tags. "Larkin, Dixon, LeBlanc, Presgraves." I turned around to Frank. He winked. We'd made it!

Frank had been dead for two days and a eulogy would be spoken, honoring a fellow officer, fallen in the battle waging in the streets of Baltimore, Maryland, aka Bodymore Murderland.

What do I say? Where do I start? I looked at the beach picture once more, and a lump came to my throat.

Chapter Four

The house was packed. The officers sat with their hats on their laps. I was standing behind a podium with my eyes on the closed coffin just below me. I looked up and saw that Daddy, J.B. and Sgt. Hawke were standing in the back. Sgt. Hawke was handing the collection box monies over to Officer Peter Niles who had found Frank's body during his tour of duty. I had put in a large check—for Marie and myself. A large donation was also contributed by the Marine Corps.

The room fell into a respectful silence. I felt the sweat prickling at my temples and gathering in my palms. I removed my hat and placed it at the edge of the podium. The outline was now in my right hand. I cleared my throat and began.

"Fellow officers and friends, I will be brief. First, let me thank all of you for your contributions." My voice escalated a step. "Detective Frank Dixon was born and raised in upstate New York, to a family that was living from paycheck to paycheck." There was no emotion in my voice. I was in control. "Early on, Frank had a strong sense of dedication—but knew that any success in his life would be accomplished only through his own efforts. Because of this, his attitude was often misconstrued as cocky . . ." There was a sympathetic rustle through the audience. "After graduating from high school with average grades, Frank joined the Marine Corps. Yet he continued to take night classes in criminal justice, hoping someday to gain enough credits to get a degree. It took him a bit longer to achieve this, because he spent a year fighting in the Gulf War. As a tank gunner, it was in the desert that he got the name 'Frank the Tank'. It was a good name, because it described his physical appearance—five foot eight inches tall, compact in build, with an open face. But don't let that face fool you. When necessary, Frank fought like a tank—fast and hard."

I hit the podium in emphasis, and my outline notes fluttered down to rest on the coffin. "Duke," Officer Jeff Stone rose from his seat up front and handed the sheet back to me.

"Thank you, Duke, but I had it memorized anyway."

"Returning from the war, Frank finished his studies to earn his degree. After several years of applying to police departments, he was offered a position to join the Baltimore City Police Department." I paused. "Baltimore was—and still is—known as one of the country's most violent cities." I heard some mild chuckling. What else? I was carrying coal to New Castle. "But to Frank, it was a challenge . . ."

"We met each other at the Police Academy during first day indoctrination and immediately felt a connection between us that grew into a bond. I was two years younger and a half-inch taller. We rented a row house together on Turnsberry Street and became roommates. Added to this, we'd both been assigned to the same district. It remained that way as we progressed through all the units of the Department, leading to the investigation of Ernest Broadway—who had been developing his drug empire under our very noses, until Frank broke the case wide open. But it's still in force despite his efforts to prevent it. He's in that coffin because of it."

"There were no witnesses to his death, no useful evidence found, no case—no anything that can remedy his life, spent and lost in another desperate war, not of his own making. The streets have finally claimed him. God bless you, Detective Frank Dixon. Soldier. Buddy. Brother." I swiftly lifted my hat, placed it firmly on my head and snapped a crisp salute. There was so much more I wanted to say—but I couldn't. The men rose as one and, hats in hand, repeated my salute. I had seen Daddy and J.B. leave soon after I'd mentioned Broadway, but Hawke kept gesturing for me to wait for him. I left the platform and went through a side door to my right, jumped into my patrol car before Hawke could prevent my leaving.

I headed toward Bel Air, a little town outside the city. In forty-odd minutes, I was surrounded by trees and long stretches of farm country. I parked my car under one of those trees, near one of those fields, and said the rest of my words I meant to say to the world.

Chapter Five

When I drove back to the Dulaney Valley Memorial Gardens, they were almost through the burial ceremony. The coffin was hanging over its final resting place. I saw Marie standing apart, under the shade of a great oak tree. She had probably rushed over before heading to the hospital for her nightshift. It was almost 4:30 in the afternoon, and the lowering sky threatened rain. As unobtrusively as possible, I joined my unit as the priest began the closing benediction.

Daddy and J.B., wearing suits, stood at the head of the line, with Sgt. Hawke next to them. Beyond them, and to their right and left, was nothing but a blur of blue uniforms. Frank had no family left, and none of his "ladies" had shown up. There was only faithful Hogan, the sole civilian to attend besides Marie. It was touching to see Hogan wearing his old police uniform, now too tight, in tribute. I could hear Taps being played somewhere as the coffin was being lowered. Suddenly, I felt like an alien among my fellow officers. Everyone started to move forward in a line. I almost turned around, as if to spot Frank behind me. We were honoring someone else's funeral, not his. As I stood there looking down at Frank's coffin at the bottom of the gravesite, I felt dizzy, then I felt Marie's hand on mine, holding me in a fierce grip.

The familiar sound of bagpipes sounded from the Emerald Society, signaling another officer laid to rest. The ranks of officers started breaking apart and dispersing. I wanted to run; I wanted to be alone.

I felt Marie following me, but I warned her with a hand signal. She understood.

Two workmen appeared through the trees, hauling their shovels to complete the job of burial. They were two stubby, middle-aged men. One of them recognized Hogan, and the three men huddled.

When I left the cemetery, the coffin itself was no longer visible. Frank was gone, but as Marie said, "He'll always be with you." So I walked us both back into life, for I knew my next step was to take possession of Frank's belongings, especially his burn box.

Chapter Six

I'd memorized the combination of the lock, just as Frank had mine. My fingers needed to drum away some time before I'd juggle those numbers: "10" to the right, "5" to the left, then "20" to the right again. The box was now my property. It had been designated as such should anything happen to Frank—and mine to Frank should anything similar happen to me. The boxes were a legacy and contained private memorabilia, unknown to one another. Once the ritual was put into motion, its contents should remain a mystery, the living custodian charged with burning the box and its contents—hence its title. It would constitute the final act of mourning for a loved comrade.

I'd decided to wait until dark before driving back to the office locker room to claim it. I doubted that Daddy had returned to his office after the burial, and the chance that other S.I.S. agents might be there was remote. We were a distant group anyway and barely ever fraternized. Too many secrets to withhold, I guess.

I waited until sunset. It was 7:30 pm before I started back to the city. As I parked, I could smell the rotting plywood in the warehouse. The walls and the sills were covered with bird shit and spider webs. My car gave a little jolt as I moved into my place, and I reached out for the white rosary dangling from the windshield—Frank's rosary, bequeathed to me—as a good luck charm. I realized it was no longer there. It had been my invisible ritual for some time—a reality I somehow had refused to fully accept until this moment. I sat immobilized for several minutes before the bird shit singed my nostrils again. I would be driving a rancid aviary on wheels by the time I left.

I entered the building proper through a large steel door, which led into a walkway where another door stood with a blank electronic keypad panel next to it. I waived my wallet containing my access card past the control panel. With a Star Trek sound effect, an array of jumbled numbers popped up on the pad. As a parting whiff of bird shit came at me, I punched a code into the keypad, and the lock release could be heard snapping open. I walked into the squad room, now shrouded in gloom. I didn't want to turn on any lights alerting anyone outside that someone was in the building. My eyes sufficiently adjusted to the darkly lit office and I made my way to the squad room. It led to the glassed-in space used for wiretapping and, across the hall from it, was the locker room. Without thinking, I switched on the light—by now not giving a shit.

Ahead of me stood twenty lockers, ten on either side with a wooden bench the length of the room. Frank's locker was at the end of the line on the right, with mine across from it. I removed my jacket and placed it on the bench. "10" to the right, "5" to the left, "20" to the right again—and there it was. I placed the box on the bench and straddle-sat behind it. In origin, it was an ordinary cigar box, with an Egyptian sphinx embossed on its cover with a couple of palm trees in the background. I looked down at it and was instantly shocked to see the tape that Frank had used to seal the box had been sliced all the way around. Had Frank hastily tampered with it? Or had someone else gotten to it before myself? Loosening the tape, I carefully opened its cover.

The first thing I saw was a photo of a naked woman. Typical Frank. It was a commercial French postcard World War II vintage. Next were five more items held together by a rubber band. Another photo, already fading—a young boy and girl with their arms around each other and self-conscious smiles on their lips. Frank and his sister as kids? Fourteen or so? The answer to the girl's identity lay under the photo—a glossy, cheap Christmas card, with the impossible home in the impossible countryside, covered in impossibly perfect snow. Merry lights beckoning from welcoming windows. "Merry Xmas, Frank. I miss you. Love, Your sister, Bea." And a date, "1997." Then followed a death notice—for Beatrice M. Eirlanger 2003—with the date and place for the funeral service. Frank had never told me about this. And what did the "M" stand for? Then, a photo of an older Frank—17 or so—standing between two grossly obese people, solemn-faced and parental. Would Frank have eventually escalated into a sad replica of his parents? So many do. If so, in that he was spared. Next, a photo of Frank a few years later, dressed in military desert camouflage fatigues, with a view of a desert behind him. This time, he had a manic look on his face, teeth bared in triumph with one hand holding a rifle, the other holding the severed head of some bearded man he'd obviously killed. At the bottom, a scrawl—"Iraq," the date and message entirely obscured. Looking at this particular photo, I could hear Frank's voice saying, "Have you ever held a man's severed head?"

We were just starting out of field training and working the same area of the city on nightshift. Frank spotted a vehicle that was driving the speed limit which in this town meant they were dirty. He had followed it for several blocks, looking for a reason to make the stop, and noticed a "felony forest"—too many scent trees hanging from the rearview mirror. Based on that, Frank attempted to stop the vehicle. No sooner did his emergency lights activate that the chase was on.

Frank did what he was trained to do. He called out his location on the radio with the plate number and description of the suspect inside. I wasn't far away.

Seconds before I came into view, I heard Frank on the radio call out that the suspect was bailing out, then the word "gun" before the radio went silent.

Just as that last transmission came through, I turned the corner and saw the suspect kneeling behind a vehicle frantically attempting to clear what appeared to be a jammed handgun. The man appeared to be of medium height, bearded, foreign looking. Frank was standing by his patrol car with his gun out and a confused look on his face. The suspect suddenly stood up and pointed his weapon at Frank. At the sight of him Frank froze. There was nothing else for me to do but run the suspect down with my car.

On impact, the dark blur of a human bounced up on my hood, breaking the windshield and damaging the emergency light bar. My car came to a sliding halt. I got out, ran to his body laying in the road behind my car. Frank stood and watched me pull the suspect's arms behind his back, causing his separated shoulders and elbows to pop and crack as if I was pulling the drumsticks of a half-cooked chicken. Seconds after I'd secured the suspect, I walked over to Frank, grabbed him, and came nose to nose. "What the hell is wrong with you? He was going to kill you." Frank's breath was steaming rapidly into the cold air. He stared at me blankly and it was then he said, "Have you ever held a man's severed head?"

Later, we sat in our booth at Hogan's—having arrived just before the shift was over, after which the place would be packed with cops looking to drown the previous shift from their memories. Frank waited until he was halfway through his Bombay gin and tonic before putting into words what was crowding his mind.

"I couldn't shoot. I just couldn't . . . not then," and his body shuddered slightly. He banged the table with his fist, then again, as if the action would stop his body's reaction to memory. When he finally spoke, his tongue was thick.

"I'd asked to be there, John. I'd been trained to be there. Although they warned me it was a very dangerous place to be—up there, on top of the tank—for everyone to shoot at, especially snipers. But, man, it was a powerful position, because you could see what you were shooting at and killing. And what was I looking for? At night, in the desert?" Frank bit his upper lip.

"I was told we were stationed at the Kuwait—Saudi Arabian borders, waiting for an attack by the Republican Guard, the best fighters they had coming our way." Frank then laughed dolefully, "I thought that was funny then. It sounded like some Star Wars army." And he kept on laughing.

"They . . . told us . . . that . . . there would be a high casualty rate and that weapons of mass destruction in the form of chemical and biological agents were most likely to be used. They put it that way. They told us that to fire us up. Instead, it scared everyone shitless. Anyway, we knew we were facing a dangerous opponent and the possibility that we were going to die. Once you accept that, the fear goes away. The will to live and protect your buddies becomes the most important thing. What the hell—what's a little poison among buddies? Bottoms up!" And seeing the already-empty glass, he wiped the inside of it with a finger and licked it. Frank was already feeling its effects.

"The tank came to a stop. And my earpiece radio keyed up, and Bunky's voice sounded from down inside the tank—something about part of a trench line in front of us, only fifty meters away. I automatically trained my gun into the darkness and waited for the attack. I couldn't see much, but what I saw was like white hands coming out of the sand, and faint sounds of Iraqi men yelling. I kept my eyes glued to those hands, and they were coming out of their trenches—hands attached to forty or fifty soldiers. I keyed my radio and let the rest of the crew know that there was a trench line of Republican Guards surrendering, and just then I heard the distinct crack of AK-47 assault rifles being fired—at our tank, at me. 7.62 caliber rounds zinging by my turret and pinging off the front and sides of the tank. Some of the Iraqis had turned around and were running back into their trenches to fight; while some others continued to stay their course toward the tank, with hands in the air. They were all mixed up together—the ones firing at us and the others' white palms up, advancing to surrender. There wasn't any question of choice. I just opened up with my .50-caliber machine gun spitting these huge flames into the blackness in front of me, cutting down the troops that were both firing at me and still trying to surrender. I could hear the sound of brass casings and link metal spewing across the tank deck, and the smell of burnt gunpowder filled the turret. Some part of me was taking comfort in that smell. It was familiar to me. It was the first time I'd killed someone and—Jesus God—it was exactly, exactly what I'd expected it to be. With the .50-caliber, people don't just get shot and stay intact. The gun is designed to rip apart its target, light armor vehicles or even buildings. But there was this guy, this Iraqi standing next to one of his own who was firing at me. Only he wanted to give up, and I pulled the trigger, and the rounds began hitting the sand in front of the man trying to give up. But my bullets moved right through him, separating his torso from his legs, ending at the soldier who was shooting at me. And I saw his head pop off his shoulders like . . . like a . . . a golf ball being hit off a tee. *I couldn't stop firing!* There were still the other targets; but I suddenly realized that there was no longer anyone shooting at me. And the people I was tearing apart were the first wave of Iraqi troops trying to surrender. I let go of the trigger when I realized this. And out there—in the distance—was a constant roar of fire as far as my eyes could see."

Frank's voice only rose in volume once. With his eyes closed, Frank went on, even more subdued than before.

"I sat up there on the top of the tank. The only move inside was to get a fresh box of ammo. I was quietly looking at and listening to the carnage I'd unleashed, draining into the sand in front of me. The bodies were spread out all around me. There was one body out there I was fixated on. He was still holding his rifle, and I kept imagining he was trying to position it so he could take a shot. So, I let a quick ten-round burst go—and later again—the same thing, that time scaring the shit out of the others trying to sleep inside the tank. But I never shut my eyes." And Frank now opened his. "I was waiting to see what I'd done up there, hoping the sun would show me it was not as bad as I had thought it to be.

"Bunky came up top at first light. He hopped off the tank, and I looked down at him on the sand. He was taking a leak, but had turned his back to what was otherwise surrounding him. I jumped off, taking my M-16 with me, and joined Bunky. My piss was vividly yellow. I pissed over the red stains of what had long since disappeared into the sand. We looked around us, wandered through the bodies—or rather body parts strewn all over. Then, there it was, a short distance away—a small dune. I gave Bunky a quick nudge. I wanted Bunky to be there with me when I looked down into the trench. And then there he was, the Iraqi soldier, his life staining the desert earth underneath him, with his head clean off. I looked around and saw a dark, round object on the other side of the trench. I walked over to it and it was the head of a thirty-something Iraqi with the Saddam Hussein mustache and all. I knelt down beside it. Its eyes were still open—not staring at me, but rolled back as if to catch a glimpse of his Muslim heaven. I shut the eyelids down against that improbable sight, then picked up the head by the hair to show Bunky. As I held the head up, blood and saliva dripped out of the burnt stub down into the sand. 'I've killed Hussein. "The war's over," I yelled. We can start heading home now.' Bunky pulled out a small digital camera—handed me my M-16—to snap a photo. Bunky asked me to lift the head up, as if I was showing off a trophy kill,'And . . . that's it . . . smile.'"

"I'm Frank the Tank, all right. But if you haven't held a man's severed head between your fingers, you haven't been to where all this is leading to . . . a once in a lifetime experience."

He slipped on the front step, and I caught him from falling on his face. We were still living together at the time. I helped him crawl up the stairs, sometimes on all fours till he made it to his bedroom. He flopped, fully dressed onto his bed and passed out. I undressed him as best I could, leaving him in his shirt and shorts.

Later, I heard some gagging sounds and found Frank with his head in the toilet bowl. I grabbed the back of his head and pulled his face out of the water, stopping him from drowning in his own vomit. It was an eerie moment. I was holding Frank's head in suspension, not unlike his grip on the Iraqi's severed head. Instead of blood, Frank sputtered water and vomit all over the floor. He suddenly galvanized himself and tore his shirt off in a single move. I could hear the buttons hitting the tile floor. Frank yelled, "Take the friggin' Iraqi off the tank, Bunky! Grab him! He'll get inside! Bunky—y!"

Frank stood stock still in the iridescent bathroom light, his naked torso glistening with cold sweats; in his mind, he was back in the desert. Then came, "I can't . . .I . . .Can't!" Then he quickly ran back to his bedroom. I found him rolled up into a ball, shivering, his sheets becoming sodden. I sat on the edge of the bed. As I did so, he lunged at me and just as quickly lay against my chest—mumbling indecipherable appeals to Bunky. I put my arms around him, and patted his back gently. I can't recall how long I did this, but at last he was still.

When I was sure he'd passed out again, I disentangled myself and covered him with the dry end of the bed sheet. It was a long time before I would shut my eyes, listening for sounds of his further distress. Frank's recall of his Iraqi ordeal back at Hogan's had been spoken with a tight control over his actual feelings—which had now spewed out of hand as he sought a vain solace in sleep.

The wild truth of what lay behind this yellowing photo before me was beyond conception. Standing by itself, it was a war relic—a penny-ante souvenir that had lost all reality.

Nobody questioned Frank on his decision to shoot that night, because there was no possible moral judgment to make. As time went on, the memory of that firefight replayed itself thousands of times over. Each time, he recalled another detail that he hadn't remembered the first time. It got to the point where Frank was not sure if his memory was playing tricks, making up things with which to plague him. For a long time after returning home to the U.S.A., Frank literally was afraid of the dark. It brought back images of that night that would often make him sick to his stomach. Frank had not fired a shot in anger since and hoped that his career as a police officer would not put him in the position again. He kept all this to himself till the night I saved his life.

I put the photo back into the burn box. There were other bits—love letters to women he'd been with. Curiously, he'd left a brand-new Kershaw knife and, under the knife, a letter addressed to me . . ."Last will and testament".

Chapter Seven

I left Frank's burn box in my locker, along with a pair of boots Frank had bought but never worn. The price tag was still attached. It was past ten before I got home. I was determined to wait up for Marie till she was off her nightshift at the hospital. The next morning, I wanted to catch Daddy at S.I.S. He could be very elusive on phone calls. I hadn't eaten all day, except for some coffee and a burnt waffle. I repeated the combination for a late-night snack. This time, I got the waffle right. I lasted another hour—reread Frank's will and passed out in the bedroom, fully dressed.

When I woke up, it was already past 7:00 am. Marie was not beside me. I tiptoed out to find her asleep on the couch, with a cup of coffee beside her on the end table. The coffee was cold, but I finished it for her—no sugar and all. I matched my lips to the imprint of her lipstick on the cup. What a pair we made. Ships in the night—much too often of late. I looked around at our apartment—a furnished rental of decent IKEA-like taste, bearing the slightly worn look of our intrepid care of it. Of course, it bore the oddments of our daily living, giving it some smattering of personal identity. It had been our home for over five years, but it was not our home. I was looking at a framed citation of mine on the bookshelf and, at that moment, couldn't recall the reason for that honor. Next to me was the photo of us on the beach—Marie, Frank and me. Feeling cramped and smelling of yesterday, I took a quick shower, changed all my gear and put on a pair of jeans and a t-shirt. I wrote Marie a brief note.

"Hey, you. I missed you and am still missing you. I'm off to see the Wizard. Can we have dinner? You're off, right? Tonight—my treat. If you're not off, fake being sick. Just this once. Please!

"See you later—

"Love you—

"Me—"

Chapter Eight

Thank God! A clean, clear morning outside, and the humidity had dropped almost precipitously. Mornings cool like this in August can always fool you for what's coming ahead.

The intrusive smell of bird shit was the first to give substance to my homily. I felt I was in a remake of some cop movie, from night to morning, as I cleared my way through the holy of holies of S.I.S.

J.B. was the first to greet me. Greet? Well, he was at least looking at me—the S.I.S. sentinel himself, whose massiveness would be intimidating at any time of day. Again, I wondered about this man. Besides chauffeuring Daddy around and doing various pickups and other such tasks, I'd never found out what J.B.'s ultimate function was. Whatever, I'm positive it contained elements of danger, made credible by J.B.'s thuggish aspect, gentled though it was by the soft voice that came out of his throat. It was almost a cloning of Daddy's own sound box, as if, on some invisible cue, J.B. slipped aside, revealing Daddy himself seated in his office.

Daddy sat behind a massive desk in his cramped office. He was in a white shirt, his jacket hanging on the tree pole by the door. Pinpoint area lights illuminated an otherwise darkened room. The walls were bare of ornaments of any kind. A bear's den. Daddy gestured for me to sit facing him while he completed some work. He was, of course, wearing his emblematic shades, impenetrable and off-setting as always. Like J.B., Daddy was a very large black man—a man burning at the long end of a long fuse. The spot shining on him lent a bluish hue to his blackness, while emphasizing the focal center of his shades. Daddy put down his pen and cracked his knuckles, which made a soft, undulant sound, matching the voice that followed. He nodded to J.B., who awaited his order to leave us alone.

"We saw you coming to join us. How did you know I'd be here?"

"I just took a chance. I needed to see you," I said forthrightly, which was ever my response to any of his questions.

"I came to see you about Frank's burn box."

Daddy leaned back in his chair.

"I have the box in my possession, as per our arrangement—Frank's and mine, that is . . ."

Daddy sat silently, waiting for me to go on.

"There is a letter in the box addressed to me, in which Frank has made me the beneficiary of all his worldly goods. Firstly, I need your authorization to get into his apartment."

Daddy nodded. "That is easily arranged. Anything else?"

"Yes, sir," I dogged on. "I was alarmed to find that the tape sealing Frank's burn box had been tampered with—in fact, broken." "John," Daddy interjected, "for a man of your intelligence and background, I'm surprised you'd even ask such a question."

"Why is that, sir?"

Daddy smiled his indulgent smile. "Dixon was the center of an investigation. Of course we opened the box—to see if there might be anything in it that could help us."

"And was there, sir?"

"None. And, unfortunately, Dixon's case is now considered cold. Is that answer enough?"

"You say 'now,' sir. Are there any plans . . . ?"

"In a year or so, the case will be reviewed by a new set of investigators from the Cold Case Squad."

"Another year?"

"John, the sooner you can get over this unfortunate turn of events, the better. Are you sure you want possession of Dixon's clothes, his whatever? The stress factor here alone must be considered. It worries me, son."

"I've already made some peace with that, sir."

"Good, but we can be helpful. Wouldn't it be better to have us dispose of his effects for you?"

"What would you do with them, sir?"

Daddy lowered his head. The gesture revealed more white hairs than I'd noticed before. He was in his mid-fifties, I thought.

"John, clothes are clothes," he drawled. "Their continued presence would only increase your sense of bitterness and regrets. My assumption is that you intend to keep them for yourself?"

"I haven't really thought . . ."

"Well, think about it, John About what I just said."

"Frank was my brother—my partner. You understand that, sir? There is no one else . . . to . . ." And I just stopped talking.

Abruptly, Daddy reached into his desk drawer and removed a sheet of paper and an envelope.

"Son, I think your attention should turn in a new direction."

"Such as, sir?"

"Yourself. I don't think you realize the level of stress you've gotten yourself in. I'm writing an order to put you on immediate stress leave for at least two months. You're too valuable to me to add any more time."

I was actually weary to even answer. He signed the form 95 memo and put it aside to get to the proper channels.

"I am sure this leave will permit you to properly deal with your period of mourning—shall we call it? The burn box itself expresses the immediacy of its purpose."

"Which is?"

"A burn box is to burn. That is its mandate and destiny. Burn it, as soon as it is possible."

"Yes, sir, as soon . . ."

"Make it sooner, John, for all our sakes. Don't linger. There has been enough suffering here." He folded the memo into three sections and placed it in the envelope.

"To malinger is to invite consequences," he added and sealed the letter, using a finger wet from a small cup to his right. He passed the letter across the desk. It had been addressed to me. The interview was clearly over. I said nothing further and started to leave, but found J.B. standing in the doorway, blocking me from doing so. Daddy's voice struck me from behind.

"John, haven't you something to give me?"

I turned back to face him again. Daddy had his hand out.

"I can't think what that would be, sir."

"Your car keys, son. You don't need one of our cars while on stress leave. That's part of the deal. They will be returned, rest assured."

"May I be permitted to return them tomorrow?"

"Why's that?"

"I promised to take Marie—my—to dinner. I'd have to explain . . ."

"Tomorrow then. You can leave them with J.B if I'm not here."

"Thank you, sir."

Chapter Nine

I drove all the way back to Bel Air, sat under the same tree I'd found yesterday during Frank's funeral and reviewed what I'd just been through. I couldn't avoid the impression that Daddy was hiding something from me. The "stress leave" tactic was a bogus ploy to keep me away from . . . ? What was "it" all about? It smelled of some kind of secret cabal against Frank. I'd been given an order to literally curtail mourning for the lost life of my closest friend and partner. "There would be consequences," Daddy had said.

It had been eight years since Frank and I had started our journey—"to save the world" in some way. And I knew I could speak for Frank in saying that, in those eight years of prolonged exposure to the violence of the streets, we'd both become numbed to it. Feelings of compassion had begun to erode, and, more and more, we'd begun to feel that nothing could surprise us anymore. I'd never held a man's severed head in my hand, but I had remembered finding a young boy who had been shot and killed only seconds before. I found him lying in the snow. There was fresh steam still coming from the bullet wounds in his head and chest that were letting the heat escape from his body, and the fresh smell of burnt gunpowder singed the crisp air. His face was expressionless, and his eyes were dimmed as if his soul had escaped through them. He had a Tootsie Pop still placed firmly in his cheek, with the stick protruding out of the corner of his mouth. The phrase "How many licks does it take to get to the center of a Tootsie Pop?" kept repeating itself in my head, as if that mattered more than the young man's life. I knew then that my soul had been damaged and that life, the most precious thing of all, meant much less since becoming a cop. The beast that separated me from the scum I hunted on those streets was staring at me, demanding entrance into my being. I knew now that only Marie could help prevent that from happening and that Frank's death must not go unresolved.

Daddy claimed that, in a year, a new cold case investigation would take place on the question of Frank's murder, but the future wouldn't change the fact that it looked like an anonymous robbery homicide. Would that yield anything other than the present judgment? A year goes so quickly, and memories and judgments fade and disappear behind vaulted walls where seeming justice is dispensed. My heart answered me. On November 12th, Frank would be 36 years old—one step into middle life. I resolved that, by that date, I would find the way to bring his death to a closure. And only on that day would I torch his burn box. This would be my final pact with my Brother. I knew, in the process,

I would be defying official orders, but that's the way this particular cookie had decided to crumble.

I stood up and looked at the incredible clarity and peace of all the pastures and open fields. I took in the supreme silence of it all and understood that my "stress leave" had taken on a real purpose. To go back—carefully back—over the path Frank and I had taken and, with the eyes of the good detective I am, ferret out what it was that led to this calamitous moment in time. Then, and only then, would I make my move. Whatever that would be.

THE
SEARCH

Chapter Ten

It was 6:01 in the morning, another blasting June day in '06. I was on my neighborhood post, sitting alone in my patrol car at the center of Cross and Carroll Streets, in the heart of Pigtown. I thought of my good parents, now in Maine for the summer, again without a proposed visit from me. While always supportive of me, my mother and father actually despised my career choice. I'd been to the best private schools, had learned to speak French and Spanish, had traveled part of the world, and had always been allowed my own options. I had been determined not to enter my father's business, Larkin Associates, men's fashion, yet still convinced in believing whatever turn I would take would be part of the plan preparing me for greatness. Now here I was, still testing the course of that destiny.

Frank was in his own car, situated less than ten minutes away. In three years, we had moved from our partnership in a shared patrol car to individual ownership of post assignments within the district. For rookies, this was a field promotion.

I looked through the window of my car onto a desolate, empty street. Not far off, one panicked junkie was walking at a brisk pace, with that familiar, frantic look of needing a fix. My car radio was on low, but my aspirations were, as always, riding high. I followed the junkie's path. He avoided my close scrutiny by ducking down a side street, dampening the possibility of being the lead to my step-up in the department.

Suddenly, my cell phone rang with a *"Dukes of Hazard"* ring tone, "Just a good ole' boy, never mean'n no harm."

"Hello?"

"Hey, it's 245. Listen, I got something for yuh."

"OK, what's up?"

"I was down the bar last night, right? And I was sittin' next to Fat Randy. He gets a call from some dude talkin' about the bricks comin' in this mornin' and that he needs to be around the way at 6:30 this mornin."

"First of all, how did you hear what the other guy was saying on the phone?"

"Fat Randy can't hear so good. He turns the cell up as far as it goes, and I was sittin' right next to him, hearin' all of it."

"Are you sure about that?"

"Hey, man, would I be callin' if I wasn't? Shit, stop wastin' my time."

"No. You stop wasting mine."

"Man, I swear that's what I heard."

"OK, so, what other details did you hear other than bricks coming in this morning? What about the location?"

"I don't know the location, but Fat Randy's hangin' around 700 Scott Street with his crew."

"Who does Fat Randy work for?"

"Beats me. But whoever it is, they got weight. Ain't nobody gonna trust some white trash Pigtown boy with no bricks unless they got some bankroll . . ."

If he wasn't right—and I started moving on what he told me—I might end up looking like an asshole. I moved out of my morning hangout to a little side street off of Washington Boulevard—a perfect spot to sit and watch cars coming into the neighborhood. So far, our informant's information had yielded diddlysquat. Small level cocaine busts, nothing to raise the temperature or catch the attention from headquarters. What got my attention about 245's call was that he was referring to bricks of narcotics, an operation being handled by someone with "bankroll". That meant there would be a special driver at the wheel—so special that, even if he was an ordinary stone-cold killer, he would be nervous about this deal and the profit he'd share if he got through to whoever was bossing it.

I was now on the lookout for that person—an unidentified guy who just didn't look right in the neighborhood, driving some vehicle of unknown make, model and color.

I looked at my watch—it was already 7:15 am. My shift would be over in twenty-five minutes. If this thing was about to happen, it was probably going to be as the shift got called in. That's the only vulnerable time when there are no police on the streets.

"9-Adam-21?"

I keyed up my radio and replied, "Nine-twenty-one," (*Shit!* I thought) "Go ahead . . ."

"Twenty-one," the dead-tired voice droned, "We have a report of a shooting in the 300 block of Annapolis Road. Caller states a black male shot by an unknown subject, no answer on the call back."

"10-4. Where does the call originate from?"

"The computer shows that the call comes from a payphone on Washington Boulevard at Cross Street."

Bingo! I immediately knew that my informant's call was on the money and that the vehicle he spoke of would be in town within minutes. "Ten-four. I'm en route." I immediately pulled out a pair of binoculars from my patrol bag and looked down Washington Boulevard toward Scott Street—in the direction where the payphone was—and spotted that white trash Fat Randy walking away from the payphone. He was now heading back toward Washington Boulevard.

I got on my cell phone and called Frank, who answered with the sound of sirens blaring, on his way to the shooting call.

"Hey! What's up, Bro?"

"Frank, ditch the siren and start making your way to Washington Boulevard and Scott Street."

Frank shut the siren off. "Why, what's up? Are you dumping this call to . . . ?"

"The call is a diversion. I need you down here ASAP. Turn your handheld to channel 3 bravo." While talking to Frank, I was trying to multitask by looking for the expected car.

"OK, Bro. I'm on my way."

Two minutes later, my handheld keyed up.

"John, you copy?"

"Yeah, Frank, 5x5. Are you in the area yet? I may have a load of dope coming to meet Fat Randy. Keep your eyes open after a vehicle and driver coming off the highway."

"I'm coming in off 395 as we speak, and I'm behind a black Crown Vic with New York tags. The driver is looking like a black male, mid-20s, and he's using his turn signals."

"Let me know if he takes the Martin Luther King exit like he's heading into Pigtown. If he does, back off. We don't want to spook him."

"10-4. It looks like he's taking the exit now. I'm going ahead. Do you have the eye when he gets off the highway?"

"I'm in a good spot to get him coming off the ramp. Take the Camden Yard exit and loop around through Ridgeley's Delight. By the way, did you see any P.C.?"

"Yeah. He's got the felony forest growing."

"John, I've lost the eye. But he's headed right down to you."

On cue, I saw the vehicle coming down the exit ramp onto Martin Luther King Boulevard, with its signal to turn left toward Washington Boulevard a good hundred yards in advance. The driver was close enough for me to see him. I didn't recognize the person driving, but I could clearly see the look of absolute fear on his face. It was the look that people have when they are so scared that they can hear their own heart beating. The driver was on his cell phone—a good sign he was giving someone the heads-up sign that he was in town. Right then, Fat Randy walked out to the corner of Washington and Scott Streets. Almost simultaneously, they both hung up their phones.

"Frank, this is the car. Get your ass over here. When he pulls up to the corner to get Fat Randy, let's box him in."

"Roger that. I'm two blocks from you. Start moving. When he slows down to get Randy, I'll come up in front of them off Calendar Street."

Like clockwork, the Crown Victoria pulled up to Randy on the corner, and the brake lights came on. I pulled out of the courtyard I was hiding in and started making my way towards them. Randy saw me coming. He opened the back door of the suspect's vehicle and jumped into the back seat, immediately lying down out of sight, as if to conceal himself from my view.

"Frank, he just picked up Randy, and they're getting ready to pull off down Scott."

"Make the stop!," Frank yelled. "Make the stop! I'm five seconds away."

I turned on my lights and pulled in behind the Crown Victoria, with my front bumper inches away from their rear bumper. Frank popped out of the small side street and locked his front bumper with theirs. It was now fight or flight, the only alternatives in this kind of scenario, for someone riding dirty.

The driver opened the car door and, staying low, maneuvered his way around it, his head swiveling to find an avenue of escape. He was following the bad-guy scenario. Even if he managed to get away, he was in unknown territory. As he kept swiveling his head to decide in which direction to run, I jumped out of my car and, within seconds, had one hand on his shirt and the other drawing my gun from the holster. I pulled the driver into me, while smacking the metal side of my Glock off the back of his head. He crumpled and fell. I had him in cuffs seconds after he hit the ground. I looked over my shoulder and saw that Frank had done something similar to Fat Randy. We had used this takedown maneuver many times before. Next, Frank started searching Randy, and called out, "Gun!" He pulled out of Randy's belt a small, black, semiautomatic handgun. I lifted my driver off the ground. He was so wiry, small that he felt like a puppet. I leaned him against my car and searched him, finding a wallet in his back pocket and a cell phone clipped to his belt. Frank and I then moved both men to the sides of our respective vehicles for a field interview. We would compare notes later.

"Hey, dude," I said, playing dumb, "Why did you try to take off? I was just stopping you to remove all the air fresheners from your rearview mirror. It looks like a regular forest, and according to the laws of Maryland, that obscures your ability to view the entire roadway safely."

"Officer, look, I ain't from around here. I just stopped to get directions from this white dude." And his eyes wandered over to Fat Randy, engaged in conversation with Frank. "He scared me, officer," my cuffed-down driver exclaimed with a kind of righteous indignation, his whining voice coming from a whining self. "I thought he was going to rob me. I was just trying to get away so you could arrest him without me being in the way." My face fell in disbelief at the staleness of his response. Oh, he was playing the bad-guy script to the letter.

"What's your name?"

"Huh?" he answered, line number four in bad-guy script. He was trying to think of what name to give.

"What—is—your—name?"

Still staring, he asked, "Who me?" He caught the look in my eyes. "Oh, sorry, officer. My name is Steven Latrell."

"OK, Steven. Is that Latrell with two *L*s?"

"No, one *L*."

This guy was a novice. "This New York State driver's license in your wallet spells it with two *L*s." Mister one *L*'s face dropped.

"Here's an easy question. How old are you?"

Another pause as he tried to remember what birth date was on his fake ID I was looking at.

"Huh?," And another "Huh? You're making me nervous, officer."

"Then stop trying to bullshit me. How old are you, God-damn-it?"

"I'm twenty-three."

"The date of birth here makes you out to be twenty-two." I was also holding Mister one *L*'s cell phone in my other hand. Without a warrant, I couldn't check the contents of the phone; but a quick look confirmed that this was the right car. The most recent call gave me a list of about ten numbers, the last call made just minutes before his arrest. The number—with a 410 area code—was indicative of a Maryland call. I pressed the *Call* button for that number, and heard Fat Randy's phone ringing in the car.

Now, Frank and I needed P.C. to either arrest them or, at least, detain them long enough to search the Crown Victoria for what informant 245 told me was in there.

Chapter Eleven

"John, what the hell? Tell me you didn't give somebody the blues! It's too early in the morning to be writing a 'Use of Force.'" This was Sgt. Hawke's opening salvo upon arriving to investigate the scene on Scott Street.

Frank and I quickly gave him a thirty-second briefing on everything that had happened in the previous thirty minutes. Hawke's eyes lit up and his clown face froze into a mask of self importance. Had he actually stumbled on a real case? Genuine curiosity spread across his face. Yes, indeedy! What was in that Crown Vic? His first move was to put in an order for two transport vehicles, one for each suspect. The idea was to keep them away from one another—to prevent any communication that might lead to more bullshit, complicating matters should the situation lead to a big case. Hawke then turned to us and, with a perfect deadpan, said, "Clock's ticking. Get to it. Call me when you're done," and he headed back to the District station.

Frank and I looked at one another, and Frank did a perfect imitation of Hawke. "What the hell are you waiting for, Larkin? Clocks ticking!" And without another word, we got to it.

We'd searched innumerable cars together and knew exactly what our respective responsibilities were. I always took the trunk. Frank searched the driver-and-passenger area. Frank was an expert in finding hidden compartments in vehicles. He had installed car stereos during the summer months when he was in high school and had a good understanding of a car's possible hidden places. In addition, as a former Marine, Frank had spent a good amount of time digging through cars at checkpoints in Desert Storm, looking for weapons.

As Steve and Fat Randy sat in separate patrol cars waiting for their rides back to the District, Frank and I began our search. Steve and Randy stared at the floor of their tight transport cages, while the cops at the wheels followed our every move.

The trunk was full of useless shit—stinky underwear, unfolded clothes and bags of old crap that didn't even belong in a garage. I pulled all of the contents out, checking every nasty pocket and shoe I could find. I was down to the last bag and had found nothing, not so much as a marijuana seed. After getting all the junk out of the trunk, I pulled the floor liner up to expose the spare-tire compartment. This was a common hiding spot for contraband because it was so well hidden under the mound of smelly clothes. Nothing! Still, I felt there was something not entirely right. Compared to the trunk of my own Crown Victoria, there seemed to be less room in this one than in my own.

I turned to look at Latrell. He was no longer staring at the floor, but had been watching me. I walked over to the patrol car he was in, opened the door, and shoved my hand inside his shirt against his chest. His heart was nearly pounding out of his chest.

I looked at Frank and, clutching my palms together, I beat them against my chest, simulating heart action. I yelled "Ka-boom! Ka-boom!"

Frank walked over and stood there between the two vehicles, looking back and forth from trunk to trunk comparing their size.

"Well, what do you know?" Frank said, almost to himself. "This trunk has been altered, dude. Right down the back wall, where the backseat would attach." He then dashed back into the suspect car and put his attention on the backseat, where the foam cushions commonly pop off with no bullying. Frank pulled the seat cushions off and yelled, "Hey, Bro!" I rushed over and looked to where he was pointing. There was a metal plate extending across the entire backseat, coming down out of the seat back. Frank tried pulling the seat back off, usually an easy move. It didn't budge an inch. Frank tried harder. Still it wouldn't move. A wicked little smile crossed his lips, and he sat down. Frank had struck gold. Not a word was said, but it was clear there was a career maker in there. "I can smell it, Bro." My deep-seated caution spoke up. "Frank," I said. "We have to reevaluate this thing . . . before we go on. If you ripped off the backseat, it won't look like we were doing an ordinary inventory—it would look as if we were really searching. At this point, the rules make it a no-no." Frank's impatience took over. "Fuck, I've got a crowbar in my trunk."

"Frank, no. We can do this by the numbers."

"I say screw the numbers!"

"And what about Hawke? If we searched illegally and find something, he'd accuse us just to have it on us and then claim ownership of the find."

"We'll call a K-9," I said. "And hopefully we'll get a positive hit on the car. With your knowledge of vehicles explaining that the backseat should have come off, we got a search warrant easy."

"Yeah, you're right," and he was himself again. He winked, and we both said it at the same time, "Get the dog!"

Chapter Twelve

Sgt. Hawke seemed in a more receptive mood when I gave him the update.

First he pondered the idea—"Larkin, as you know, I know about everyone in the department, as well as which K-9 is worth the department's Puppy Chow. Get the prisoners off the street, while I find a dog worth a shit."

"Thanks, sir," I said respectfully.

"There'd better be something to all this," Hawke grumbled. "You know you broke the unwritten rule of shift work."

"Not quite, sir," I answered, still respectfully.

"What do you mean 'not quite'? No one in their right mind makes a car stop that close to shift change."

"I . . . just had this hunch, sir."

"Fuck hunches!" he balked. "We're going to have to go through a lot of shit because of your hunches, not to mention pay overtime."

I didn't say anything.

It was 7:30 am when the K-9 SUV pulled up to the scene. The Crown Vic had been brought to the sally port garage at the District station where the search would continue under official scrutiny. The dog, a three-year-old German shepherd named Riggs, was already barking up a storm from his cage in the SUV.

Frank nudged me in the shoulder. "Damn, that dog's good. He can smell it from up there."

I still felt nervous, a state not alleviated by what I saw happening around us. A small crowd of officers of various ranks was gathering. If Riggs found nothing, Frank and I would have to suffer public humiliation besides official censure. The K-9 officer stepped out of his truck and approached us. A small,

43

burly man, he looked as if he had slept in his clothes. We could smell him coming.

"Hey, how's it going?" he said in a gravelly voice. Riggs was still to be let go.

Mr. K-9 turned and said several authentic-sounding German phrases to Riggs, then addressed us again.

"Are you two the troublemakers with the 'secret compartment' theory? Officers Larkin and Dixon, right?" Frank turned away.

"Right so far, sir." I looked around to see how many officers had heard him. Frank pursed his lips, gave me a subtle wink and answered in his most serious mode for this geezer.

Frank said, "Yes, sir. We're just looking for some P.C. for a warrant."

I added, "The backseat looks like someone did some customizing for a compartment, sir."

Mr. K-9 took one look at the backseat, and the anticipation of getting Riggs in there could be seen crossing every inch of his crusty face. He couldn't be more than thirty. K-9 officers get credit for the busts their dogs make, and this officer clearly saw a doggie commendation coming his way. On command, Riggs jumped out of the back of the SUV, head raised, sniffing the fresh air, assessing the situation. He looked at the people standing around, including two police officers who had just arrived, but who immediately jumped back into their cars. Riggs preened smartly—his nose twitching rapidly in the direction of the backseat—and, like a wily stalker, moved toward the car. One deep growl and he jumped into the car, looking intently at the backseat cover, as if he could see right through it. Mr. K-9 blurted out some word in German that must have meant "Go get it!" With his eyes still on the seat, Riggs bared his fangs and began tearing at the cushions, as though tearing flesh from a bone. After a grisly couple of minutes, the K-9 officer resumed shouting commands. The dog reluctantly stopped thrashing at the backseat cover, already ripped, shredded, and otherwise destroyed. Mr. K-9 looked at Frank and me.

"I haven't seen Riggs freak out like that in a long time. Boys, you must have hit the jackpot on this one," he said with a self-congratulatory leer.

When I looked at Frank, his face had taken on an intense expression. He walked quickly toward the car. I immediately followed, as did Mr. K-9. Frank paused before entering the vehicle, as Riggs, on another command, leapt out and went to his master's side, his breathing hard, his frothy saliva dripping to the ground like beer suds. Mr. K-9 kneaded the animal's back in praise, feeding him a treat. Frank slowly removed his jacket, which Hawke, stepping up at the ready, took into personal custody. In his fingers dangled the warrant, permitting us to "get on with it." Frank then slowly climbed into the backseat to study the punishment Riggs had inflicted on its cushions. The gathered crowd stopped its buzzing to silently watch the man who had replaced the German shepherd.

Riggs was now sitting proudly on his haunches, still breathing heavily. His was the only sound to be heard in the garage. Frank rummaged in the debris scattered all over the car. Finding nothing, he fixed his attention to the underbelly Riggs had exposed, and stared, as if he was meditating over the ruins before him. Like Riggs, he could see beyond the ravagement.

Riggs piped up with a few barks. Frank turned to us.

The intensity on his face had not diminished. No more high-jinx here. It was extraordinary what a chameleon this man was.

After a couple of seconds, Frank said, "There has to be some latch release code to open this." He picked up a shred of cushion seat to smell, like some secret was locked in it. He then looked outside the car, as if to where the secret had eluded him and fled. He saw the crowd watching him. Now choice with officers and higher-ups, united in their grave attention.

Frank spoke out loudly, "Riggs has done his work and done it well. Now it's up to us!"

Hawke, still holding Frank's jacket, chimed in, "You heard the man." Then to Mr. K-9, "Why don't you go back to your dog? He looks lonely." And with a studied gesture, Hawke wrapped Frank's jacket over his arm like some maitre d' at a classy hotel. Frank followed his first supposition with another. "There has to be a system here—some buttons or knobs to be pushed in a specific order for the compartment to unlatch." Frank dropped the cushion patch, backed into the car, and tried to see it in a fresh light. First, he turned the car's headlights on, then methodically pushed the overdrive button. Lastly, he sat behind the steering wheel and tilted it all the way down. He raised his head, as if listening for something, then turned to look at the backseat again. Nothing had changed.

"I could poke around and press this and that and still not find the answer," he said in quiet resignation.

"We need to find the wires and close the circuit."

"Well, what the hell," Mr. K-9 interceded.

"If I let Riggs back inside, he'd have everything dismantled in no time."

There was an anticipatory smile on his face. Frank continued on with his own deductions. "We've got to find the wires—that's the important factor. The one good thing about this kind of lock system is that it relies on some sort of electrical circuit being opened for the compartment to stay shut. What I need is a set of gator clips and a car battery."

"Small jumper cables," I said to clarify. Mr. K-9 looked totally bewildered. Dogs were obviously his total bailiwick.

"Frank," I suggested, "You go ahead and find the wire. I'll get the tools you need," and I quickly made my way back to my own car. Once there, I removed the car battery and, in doing so, found one of the District Drug Units that had a set of gator clips handy. By the time I returned to Frank, he had pushed up his shirt sleeves and dug through several inches of carpet and foam to find the wires. I could see the wires were a non-factory blend and had rested far too deep in the car to be there for legitimate purposes. Frank put down the wires and took all the materials I'd brought him. He was like a surgeon attending an ailing patient, moving with precision and quiet confidence.

At this point, the District Commander filtered into the carport to witness the exhumation of a possible career seizure. Now my heart was clearly booming. As Frank hooked up the last of the gator clips, his eyes sought mine to exchange a silent signal, and he closed the circuit. As soon as the connection was complete, a slow humming sound could be heard coming from the trunk of the car. At first, nothing happened. Then, as if a tomb had been unearthed, the entire backseat sat up and shot forward with long hydraulic pistons leading the way. Almost immediately, everyone surrounding the vehicle started applauding. There appeared to be a foam liner covering the contents of the cavern. Without hesitation or concern for preservation of evidence, Frank pulled away the liner, exposing the neatly packed, square packages consistent with the size and shape of kilogram bricks of narcotics. There was an eruption of general cheering, with the wild yelping of Riggs overriding the enthusiasm. Sgt. Hawke had a "holy shit" look on his face. His eyes positively twinkled, while his right hand automatically brushed Frank's jacket, still resting over his left arm. Riggs' yelping receded into the distance as Mr. K-9 pulled the reluctant dog back to their SUV.

Most of the cops who had gathered to watch had never seen narcotics greater than the small amount that would cause a street-level dealer to run. This was, by far, the biggest seizure that the District had ever seen.

Knowing this, Frank dove down out of the car into my arms, and we gave each other mammoth bear hugs, realizing we had just punched the tickets out of the bag and into at least a district level knocker unit. The District Commander gave us his final "atta boys," as the spectators began leaving. The hubbub, back slaps and general delirium quickly spent their force. It was time for us to meticulously collect the evidence and submit it with the requisite paperwork, making sure we'd crossed all the *t*'s and dotted all the *i*'s. Hawke ceremoniously raised Frank's jacket, and Frank shimmied into it. The ferocious beam on Hawke's face had also never been seen before ever in the district—I'd swear to it. Hawke shook hands as if the operation had been masterminded by his own self and the result a personal triumph.

Chapter Thirteen

With the ebbing of the crowd, Hawke now became his old, beloved self. Deciding it would be best to call the crime lab down to the scene to fingerprint the entire vehicle, including the ten kilo packages, before they were even removed from the no-longer-secret compartment. It was clear to everyone involved that this case was going to reach out far beyond the borders of Baltimore, including, without a doubt, to the United States Attorney's Office.

As every good politician knows, there is nothing better than calling a press conference. In the Baltimore cop world, it is best with dope and guns on the table. The brass love showing off this kind of stuff to the media. It makes them appear as though they are running the department efficiently and that the current seizure was an action led, of course, directly by them. Commonly, when a newsworthy bust comes along, the officers are "asked" to join the dog-and-pony show and smile for the cameras. We showed up on time at the headquarters Public Information Office. When we walked into the room, we saw a neat display on the table closest to the podium of the ten kilos that were found inside the vehicle along with the gun taken from Fat Randy.

As the film crews arrived to set up their cameras and other equipment, several of the local news personalities were taping their preambles to the story. We just stood silently out of the way, as if we had nothing to do with what was going on. Commanders filtered in, walking past us as if we were there to serve coffee, and greeted other commanders like they hadn't seen them in a while. I noticed a tall, thick man with an extremely dark complexion and neatly trimmed cornrows walk into the room. He didn't acknowledge the other commanders and he didn't appear to have a police ID card showing, which struck me as odd since it is mandatory for all non-uniformed personnel when inside the building. He slowly checked out the news crews to make sure they weren't filming and then he approached us as we stood against a wall.

"Hey, boys, come with me for a sec." We had no idea who this guy was, but he appeared to know who we were, unlike anyone else in the room. We followed the tall black man out of the pressroom and down the hall to a break room that was guarded by another black male who looked as though he had just stepped off a dope corner. He didn't have an ID either.

The three of us walked into the room, with the man stopping to whisper something to the guard before closing the door behind him. I was thinking to myself that these guys had to be feds and that they were there to tell us that we had arrested an undercover DEA agent with ten kilos and that they would handle the case from there. I saw red at the idea. Instead, the man sat down at the table, motioned for each of us to join him and handed us individual sheets of paper. At closer inspection, they turned out to be transfer requests—requests already signed by the Police Commissioner and even filled out with our names, social security numbers, etc., all but our John Hancocks. We looked over the forms, specifically trying to find the portion that reads "Duty Assignment Location". In that block were three letters, "S.I.S". I looked at the man who had brought us there, not knowing who this guy was or even how to address him, and asked a perfectly sensible question, 'Sir, what exactly is S.I.S?' With no expression on his face, the mystery man simply stated, 'Son, S.I.S is a unit within a unit, Special Forces of this agency that operate outside the box. If you are interested, sign those transfer orders, and it's done. But you won't be fully briefed until you sign those papers." Before I could even think of another question to ask, Frank was pulling out his pen and scribbling his signature at the bottom of the form and said, "John, sign the paper. We won't get this offer again."

I knew that I would sign the form from the minute it was given to me, but I didn't want to seem too anxious. I'd been so . . . for so long . . . and after all, I still didn't know who this guy was. I took the pen from Frank, stared at the form for a minute to make it look like I was still making up my mind, playing a grateful shit liar, and finally signed it. "Good, then. First thing tomorrow morning, a squad member will pick you up at your houses. In the meantime, bag up all your departmentally-issued items—uniforms, pants, shirts, boots, everything—and bring them with you. And not a word to anyone about this. Good job, guys. Welcome to S.I.S."

The gentleman stood up and left the room. The guard was quickly on his heels. Frank and I, suddenly stricken by the same thought, simultaneously yelled out, "Shit!" While processing with the S.I.S, we had missed the opportunity of being filmed by the camera crew. All because that unidentified man had called us away from the filming. The first guy was, of course, J.B., who would be formally introduced later. Frank lightened the burden of a chance missed. "Bro, ease up. There'll be other occasions," he winked. "Let's go get a drink."

Chapter Fourteen

What had started as another sultry day in the confines of the Southern District had escalated so that the weather colluded to extol us. The sun appeared and spread itself on a carpet of cool air that suddenly embraced a city badly in need of embracing. Time for a little drink indeedy. At 5:45 by the clock, Frank and I took ourselves over to Hogan's Alley, where our entrance was greeted by another salvo of *Bravos*. We cut a swath through a full house of cheering cops.

"Sit down, boys," Hogan said. "You two assholes look like you could use some refreshment." We sat in our favorite booth, drinks already in place.

Hogan praised on, "I heard about your seizure this morning. Goddamn, you're making everyone else look bad!" At that, we rose and lifted our glasses to the boys—a Bombay gin and tonic for Frank and a Jim Beam Black with Diet Coke for me. Hogan stood there clapping his hands, his sixty-odd years at attention, blue eyes sparkling, and his gray, wavy hair exuding whiffs of Brilliantine.

Frank leaned toward me. "Don't look," he said, "but I think some of the saddlebags are about to drop to the floor, they're hammered." Frank was referring to the saddlebags hanging off the gun belts of some of the officers addicted to carbonated barley and hops. Hogan blessed us like a presiding bishop and left to attend to the clambering saddlebags—brothers—who had been in the service way before our time.

There is something almost therapeutic about the first sip of an alcoholic beverage after a crazy shift. It's almost as if that one sip opens the mental floodgates that let all the tensions run out of you. My second salute was to the wall beside us, peppered by the faces of our comrades, going back to the eighties, when Hogan first opened his bar. Frank and I would be looking down, too, one day.

"Frank, do you think it was deliberate?"

"What was?"

"Our being taken out of the room, before the cameras could . . ."

"Yes, of course," he said.

"Why?" I responded angrily.

"They want all the credit. The department does. Besides, if we're about to become part of S.I.S, that means personal anonymity as far as we are concerned."

At that precise moment, I heard a gunshot and everyone's heads suddenly lowered in unison, then Hogan's angry voice shouting at one of the officers, "You asshole, you! Hand it over! Come on, hand it over, Mulvaney."

Frank and I stood up to see what was happening. Hogan had ducked under his bar and pulled out his big lockbox and placed it on the bar. Mulvaney, an officer who towered over the diminutive owner, could only offer an apologetic bleat. "We were just celebratin' the boys' achievement, that's all, Hogan."

"By putting a hole in my ceiling?" And Hogan looked up at the possible damage and began fuminating, "Great, just great. The shot probably went right through the bathtub upstairs in my apartment. You'll pay for the damages, Mulvaney. Meanwhile, take your gun out of your holster and put it in the lockbox. And that goes for the rest of you if you're entertaining similar ideas!"

Hogan grabbed the key dangling from a hoop around his neck. "You'll only get your gun back when you leave." And he lifted the lockbox to Mulvaney, who complied by placing his pistol in it.

"Jesus, Hogan," Mulvaney moaned, grabbing his now-empty holster. "I feel naked!"

"That's the house rule, and you know it is. In fact, for safety's sake, I want all the rest of your unit to do the same." An uproar went up around Hogan, aided and abetted by a group of officers standing outside the pool hall part of the pub, raising their pool sticks like a bunch of aborigines about to attack.

"Shut your traps!," Hogan's flinty voice roared. There was instant silence. That's when Frank took advantage of the lull and yelled, "Hogan! My darlin' friend, Hoge, let's not spoil the day. I'm up for a round on us, for the whole room." Everyone cheered again in relief. I suddenly looked dismayed. Frank caught my expression.

"Come on, dude," he cajoled. "It's only money. And I'll make it up to you." Hogan quickly leapt on the gauntlet, weighing both the huge, unpaid tab already accrued by Frank and the marvel of the day's achievement. The latter won.

"I'll go with that," Hogan shouted, "and it's on me, to honor Frank and John, proper like. Now, how about that?" And harmony was restored.

"Now can I have my gun back?" Mulvaney almost pleaded.

"Only after I check my tub first!" And squinting at Mulvaney, Hogan rushed to fulfill his investigation upstairs.

"Well, you got away with that one . . . thanks to Hogan."

"C'mon, Bro, what's money?"

"It's only money," I imitated his singsong in response.

"You know I'll make good."

"You create soft places in peoples' hearts—not to mention their pockets. How do you get away with it?"

"I said I'd pay it all back. Don't you believe me?"

"I trust you, but, right this moment, Bro . . . no, I don't believe you."

He winked, made a sad face, then winked again. What confidences are allowed when buddies are deeply in their cups. Then came Frank's inevitable sequel, "Females to be gathered and conquered to complete the day's victory."

Chapter Fifteen

. . . .

Thinking of Marie on her night shift, I swore this would be my last "Honey Hunt," as Frank called them, all accomplished via the internet. But today's deserved high was hard to repress. Frank was sitting in the front seat of his car with a laptop; I in the backseat, looking over his shoulders at the promising parade of rentable beauties.

"Wait," I said, while scanning the candidates. "Pull back to the one we just saw." A beautiful blonde, wonderful credentials, etc., but . . .

"Hey, Bro, what's up? You're not falling in love?," Frank chided.

"Love? Look!," I said.

"I'm looking."

"At her left shoulder."

"I don't see anything, Bro."

"Yes, you do. You know how I feel about tattoos on women . . ."

"Tattoos? Where?"

"Look close."

"Oh. Maybe it's part of a mole?"

"Mole, my ass."

"A beauty mark then."

"Maybe," I faltered sheepishly.

"Can I move on now?," Frank said and punched in the next darling.

"Speaking of moles, have you seen Marjorie Wyatt lately?"

"I haven't seen Marjorie since the 4th of July. But she'll show up in time to bring me my Christmas present."

"How can you be so sure?"

"Well, to quote a cherished friend, at last sight of her, there was no indication on her remarkable body that she'd confined me to off limits. I'm still on her list of considerations."

"Considerations? For what?"

"I'm being, as they say, discreet, Bro, but I believe you can handle the confidence." Frank was in his Cary Grant mode.

"Spill it."

"Until another, more impressive wang comes along during her journey through life, mine will be elected to grace her form."

"By 'wang', are you referring to your dick?"

"'Peter' is the preferred expression, Bro . . ."

"Well, when she gives you the OK, will there be a party with an unveiling?"

"Possibly."

"Will you be posing for her or does she work from a photo?"

"From memory, Bro, memory."

"Click! Smile for the camera."

"You're being cruddy. Real cruddy."

"I tend to, when drunk," and I smiled my best smile.

"Well, stop busting balls and get on with this. Times a' wasting! One more remark, and I'll rat on you with you-know-who!" And he was capable of that, in his wacky way. "How about this one?" And he pointed to the screen. But being in the vein, I busted on.

"You know, there's something almost sacramental about Marjorie coming back into your life over and over . . ."

"Bless you, Father John, now knock it off."

"No, honestly. It's like her coming back on pilgrimage. You are a regular, walking Holy Grail, you are."

"Look, I don't like bashing religion. I may not be a believer anymore, but I believe in the idea. Ah-the rosary" I said, "Now I understand."

By now, several of the men had left Hogan's and made their way to Frank's car. The "pick of the crop" show was always an attraction.

They hung around, pitching for their choices with whistles and moans—and various shades of envy, jealousy and loneliness, to which we were all susceptible. The street was a harsh taskmaster, especially for mostly bachelor gentlemen who knew no other way of life and only the temporary refuge of soft arms.

Frank and I would go back to our respective digs, shower, shave and change to meet the chosen beauties in the lounge of one of the better hotels. There, Frank would flash his badge at the concierge, who would immediately assign us to one of their empty suites with champagne that would last until the wee hours. Whether the night afforded total bliss or made no difference. It was the glamour of it all that mattered. The extra dollop lay in that it had been illegally achieved and not cost a cent, but for decent tips to the bartender and the concierge. Frank loved the conceit of it all. That he lived beyond his means goes without saying, but he was driven to fulfill his dreams. Toward that end, he would beg, borrow—even from the ladies—but never steal; continually promised restitution that never came; and everyone in this scenario loved him. Being an irresistible charmer, we all forgave him and looked forward to the next caper of this Errol Flynn of the Southern District. Now, with Marie in my life, these love parades were no longer tenable for me, I kept promising myself I would muster the nerve to tell Marie about them. Or will that effort to confess be like the tabs Frank never paid? Last "chick folly" or not, Frank and I had turned the hoped-for corner with our K-9 bust. The shadow that would fall over it all was being simultaneously prepared in the wings.

THE
INVESTIGATION

Chapter Sixteen

· ·

"Welcome to S.I.S," J.B. said, with what looked like some genuine smile on him.

"S.I.S, my ass," I said under my breath. Then I saw him—the other black man who had met us at the dog-and-pony show. Daddy? Who else? All natty in a gray silver suit and tie, he went to J.B.'s side, whispered something and patted his back while leading him to the office door so that Daddy could be alone with us. This was all synchronized choreography. The main door shut, and Daddy turned to us with a benign expression and indicated for us to choose what would become our desks. Frank had already chosen his and was seated at it. I took the desk right across from him, while Daddy planted a chair between us. Suddenly, we became two students in attendance to their teacher. It was a kindergarten of sorts after all.

Staring at us through his light colored shades, he said in a confident voice, "This is the most operationally secure unit in the agency. I have read both your personnel files, and I must say that, with the short amount of time you guys have on, they are quite impressive. Until now, you guys have been doing good work as patrolmen, but now it's time to kick it up a couple of notches. There are some things you need to know about S.I.S. The Special Investigations Section falls directly under the Police Commissioner himself. No other command staff member oversees this unit, because most of them don't know it exists. We are the smallest unit within the agency, yet we are the most heavily funded. We operate with the money we make during our investigations and what's left over from homeland security grants. We also cross-designate and deputize with federal agencies to allow us a bigger playing field. You guys will operate within a squad, working one case at a time. Each squad within this unit is sciffed off from each other to avoid case contamination. All evidence is stored at this location, all reports are done in-house and never leave this building and all operations go through me. From here on, I'm your new Daddy. If you need anything to do your jobs—whether it is money, clothes, cars—you come to Daddy. Am I being clear so far?"

We almost simultaneously sounded off, "Crystal, sir."

"This type of work, if not done right, will get people killed. The most important thing for you guys to adhere to is keeping your mouths shut. Your friends and families cannot know what you are doing, your old coworkers that you suck drinks back with after shift cannot know what you are doing, whoever you two are sticking your dicks in cannot know what you are doing. Take this any way you want, but if I find out that you compromised this unit, I will bury you. That being said, give me your credentials."

We pulled our police credentials from our back pockets and handed them to Daddy.

"Traditionally, police have taken the chase approach to major narcotics investigations. They often do cases that lead to some organized middlemen getting pinched for the crime, while the real moneymakers—the bosses—get off. Police tend to make it their mission to chase the narcotics, making investigative guesses about where and when it's gonna' be so that they can swoop in and make the seizure in time for the eleven o'clock news. Here, we set it up so the narcotics come to us. Let me ask you a question—when it comes to making a profit off of narcotics, where is most of the risk taken?"

I spoke up, "Trusting people within the organization enough to keep their mouths shut and not rip you off."

"To an extent, yes, but that answer is wrong. The biggest risk, when it comes to trafficking narcotics, is transportation. The people that oversee the shit getting from point A to point B take the most risk and have the most to lose when they get popped with, let's say, ten kilos. You boys—with your ten-kilo caper—have created an opportunity. These ten kilos are most likely a small portion of what they have been regularly bringing in. Your first case is going to be taking advantage of the circumstances that you created with this car stop yesterday. You're going to make the dope come to you. Follow me so far?"

In an attempt not to seem as stupid as I felt after my answer to Daddy's first question, I merely nodded that I understood. Frank kept his mouth shut and followed my lead.

"This is the game plan. As we speak, our people have taken custody of your new friends, Steve and Fat Randy. You will interview both of these guys and try to learn what kind of volume they have been bringing in. Find out what types of transportation they use, who they deliver to, but more importantly what kind of influence they might have on the person they report to. Most of the details about who those bosses are and where the bricks are coming from is not something these two low men would know about. They may claim to know, but they don't. Report back to me when you're done so we can reevaluate things. Any questions?"

I jumped at the opportunity. "Daddy, sir?" (I couldn't believe I was calling this man "Daddy"). "Aren't we starting the Q and A with a strike against us?"

"Namely?"

"Well, the media has already made it news."

"Latrell and Fat Randy have been kept from public exposure. The media does not know they exist. For their good and ours, they have been given a scenario—briefly, that they managed to escape, abandoning the vehicle, and have been living in out-of-town motels until this blows over. Whoever they are working for knows no more or less."

"And when they eventually come out of hiding?"

"We will supply them with bona fide rental and food bills from the various establishments for their alibis. All personnel involved will be bonded to this scenario. Now, I'll be seeing you boys later. Meanwhile, J.B. needs to go over several things with you."

Frank and I were still at our desks as Daddy rose from his chair, replaced it, then came and shook our hands and left the office. On cue, J.B. came down the hallway passage.

"Things making a little more sense? Well, open your desk drawers. You'll find your keycards to get into the building. The codes are on a sticky note in back. Commit the code to memory and then shred it."

I looked around the room and asked, "Where is the rest of the squad?" J.B. muttered. "We have ten guys on the squad; us three plus one more is with the city, two from DEA, two from FBI and two from ICE. The two DEA guys are in Afghanistan until next week. If all goes well, they'll get here just in time. The next step is for you to pick cover names for yourselves, using your actual first name, adding to it a fictitious last name. If you can't think of a name, think back to high school and pick the last name of an old girlfriend. Here is a list of abandoned houses that you can use for addresses."

61

Daddy suddenly reappeared at the door of his office and beckoned J.B. to join him.

"Use the time, boys. Waste not, want not!" And J.B. went into Daddy's office, and the door closed.

Frank swiveled around in his chair, his face beaming, "I've been dreaming of this moment. From lonely patrolman to undercover knocker."

"So have I," I chimed in. "You've picked one already, too?"

"Yup. Frank Stevenson," he said grandly. "Now how's that sound? Has a ring to it," and he repeated the name. "The ladies will love it. What's yours?"

"John Celestini," I answered. "It's my mentor's name back at Northeastern University," I explained. "Wait a minute," I suddenly added. "You did say 'Frank Stevenson'?" Frank stared at me.

"I did," and he swiveled again.

"Bro, I hate to disillusion you, but there is already a certain Frank Stevenson."

"Is he famous?"

"You bet."

"You see," and Frank beamed again.

"He's a famous porn star," I said. Frank stopped swiveling. "His actual name is unpronounceable Polish, but he's known to the world as 'the Pole with the pole.'"

"Don't shit me . . ."

"I shit thee not. Check him out on your computer."

But J.B. returned briskly, speaking as he approached, "All right, guys, we have a lot of shit to get through today, so let's move it!"

Chapter Seventeen

The federal courthouse is a large building that takes up an entire square block. The building is a combination of gray stucco and white marble, the windows are tinted, and there is a half-decent attempt at landscaping outside the front entrance.

We had been here before, but not under these circumstances. We followed the narrow driveway down under the building and came to a split in the road where another guard was posted. The guard pointed to a small elevator near the gun lock boxes. We entered the small prisoner transport elevator and went up to the third floor. We got off the elevator where we were greeted by Daddy and a lady he introduced to us as "Jennifer" standing in the hallway having a conversation.

"Thanks for getting here on time, boys. We have two interview rooms set up for you, both of which will be observed by me and Jennifer"—with no further explanation about who Jennifer was.

"Who do you want to go at first?" I already knew that we would have a better chance at the prize if we talked to Fat Randy first.

"We'll take Randy first. He's a soft white boy. I'd like to get some intel on who they're working for before we go at Latrell." Daddy gave me a half-smile, like he agreed with my logic.

"Good choice." Daddy opened his Nextel phone with the two-way talk button and requested the guard to bring Randy up.

"Jennifer will be working on this case—you'll see how." And mysterious Jennifer then took over.

She led us to the interview rooms on the same floor as the prisoner booking station. She walked inside of a room with a small sign hanging on it that said "Interview in Progress". There were two other doors flanking the one we just entered that said the same thing. We entered the room; it was dimly lit, with two large one-way glass panes on either side. On the other side of the glass were two interview rooms. One was empty. The other had Latrell sitting at a table alone, wearing the same clothes that I had arrested him in. He must have felt the vibration from the door closing, because he looked up at the mirrored glass, as if he could feel us looking at him. He had the look of someone who was angry—I figured two days in isolation could do that to you. Besides angry, he looked haggard and hungry, and I could smell the putrid urine and sweat of city jail through the glass. Lack of sleep or food had to be tactics Frank was accustomed to in Iraq. It would also be the gateway to our interrogation. Frank looked around. We were alone.

"Jennifer," he said, "those legs never stop. How high the moon, Bro?"

"I know the type," I said. "A sexy lady lawyer, reserved by day, but wild by happy hour."

"Does Daddy have his lady friends involved?"

"I doubt it, but then who knows? She's got a D.C. swagger about her. A Condoleezza Rice type, only in a skirt. Don't get any ideas." I turned away to find Jennifer standing there again. Had she heard our little appraisal of her? You would not suspect it from her manner.

"Gentlemen," she said, "a little last P.S. Daddy asked me to deliver. Make sure you ask Randy if he knows anything about 'lappers.'"

We both said, "What?"

"Lapper. L-A-P-P-E-R. Try to remember." She scanned over both of us and vanished again down the corridor.

I turned to Frank and mumbled, "Did you get that, LAPPER?" Frank put out his tongue and, with it, lapped the air around him.

The sound of leg irons being dragged down the linoleum hallway grabbed our attention. The door to the second interview opened, and Fat Randy, being escorted by the guard, entered the room. There were three chairs in the room, two of which were facing the door and a lone chair facing the wall. The positioning of the chairs was perfect. Commonly, when people are going to lie, they look for something in the room to focus on instead of the interrogators. The guard uncuffed Randy, but left the leg shackles on, then instructed him to have a seat. As if he knew his place, Randy took the lone seat facing the wall.

Jennifer appeared again and beckoned us forward. She looked at us and said, with great deliberation, "All right, guys, do what you do. Our main goal is to gather as much intel as possible and get him to agree to signing a contract with the Department of Justice that he will cooperate and testify." Frank piped in with the same question that I was going to ask.

"So, what can we offer him in terms of a deal?"

Jennifer, anticipating the question, stated, "Don't offer anything. Once he agrees to work with us, I will come in and go over the specifics of his agreement. Just get him on board."

Frank and I looked at each other and, with a clear mission, walked out to the hallway. We stopped briefly before going into the room with Randy and gave each other a quick fist bump. I walked in first. With the sound of the doorknob turning, Randy swiveled in his seat to see who was coming in. His face was very red from the anticipation of what was going to happen. His hair was matted, like he'd been sleeping on a metal bed for a few days. Frank and I took our seats across from him as he moved back into his seat, staring at us both. There was a moment of silence before Frank spoke.

"Good to see you again, Randy."

Randy's eyes jumped back and forth between us as he softly responded, "Yeah, so, what's this all about?"

I said, "Randy, do you know where you are right now?"

Randy quickly responded, "Yeah, I'm at the courthouse."

I elaborated on the question, "That's right, but do you know which courthouse you're in?"

"I don't know the name of it, but I assume it's the federal one. I saw the big sign out front when we pulled in."

"That's correct, Randy, you're in the federal courthouse. I wanted to make sure that you knew the full circumstances behind why we're sitting here and that the case in which you're involved is no longer being handled by the State's Attorney's office." Randy's eyes widened in horror.

This point was very important to make out of the gate—the thugs on the street have no respect for the Baltimore City State's Attorney's Office, which is pretty much amateur hour all the time. The one judicial system that they are afraid of being prosecuted in is federal court.

With that out of the way, I started my "coming to Jesus" speech, just in case he thought that wasting our time would prolong his absence from a cold cell.

"All right, Randy, you know why we're sitting here, and you know that the amount of coke, along with the gun, can land you in some federal prison—God knows where—for the rest of your adult life. Everyone has a defining moment in their life, where they have to make a decision that will impact the rest of their life. This moment is yours. The good thing for you is that you have a few cards to play in this card game. The big decision is if you want to stay in the game or fold. Before you answer that question, I want you to think about your family, your girlfriend, your friends and yourself. I want you to think about all the good times you have had as a free man and ask yourself one question: 'Am I ready to give my life up for someone else that doesn't give a shit about me?'"

"I can't go to jail, man." He started breathing heavy, and his color visibly changed. "I ain't the big fish and sure as shit ain't takin' a hit for these hood rats. I just want you guys to know that I am nobody in this deal. My job was just to get the load to our people in Pigtown and do security while they cut it up. I don't have shit for money, and the gun wasn't even mine—one of the corner boys gave it to me just in case."

I thought to myself that this was easier than I thought it would be, so decided to go right at the prize. "Whose bricks was this that you were doing security on?"

His eyes welled up, and his head sunk into his lap. Through his sobbing, Randy quickly spit it out.

"It was Broadway's, man. It's Broadway's. He runs all this shit down in Pigtown. From Westport to MLK, he's got the market."

I wanted to keep him talking.

"OK. Tell me more about the operations." Randy looked away and started to moan. It was a crucial moment for us.

"There's no going back, so what else would you gain by holding back?"

His fat underbelly of a face was getting even whiter.

"Calm down, Randy. Let's just take it in small chunks." Randy's hands did flip-flops on his lap.

"First tell us about how you know Lattrell."

Randy sighed heavily, "I don't know about him, but I know he's a big player for Broadway."

"How big?," Frank eased Randy on.

"He sets up the packages coming from NYC."

"Had you ever worked with him before?," I took over from Frank.

Randy's hands flopped again, "Nope. This was the first time."

Frank prodded, "OK, tell us everything you know about Broadway."

"That son of a bitch!" Randy suddenly yelled in absolute fury. "He's a power hungry motherfucker, man. He's like them foreigners who send kids into big machines to grease them up, then accidentally turn the machines on when they're still inside—," and he began making guttural sounds of disgust, with self-loathing sounds and more disconnected invectives against Broadway.

"OK. Whoa, Randy, whoa," Frank and I cajoled. "One thing at a time. Let's go back to the beginning. We need—"

"Screw what you need! It's what I need!"

"And what is it that you need?" I asked.

"I—I—need—I need . . . something to eat, is what I need. Right now! I'm growling so bad my insides hurt. I don't want to go on with any more stuff. No sir! No sir!"

"There is no need to shout," I said quietly.

"Yes, there is! I can't hear for shit, and I want to be sure of what I'm saying, right now, I'm saying I'M HUNGRY!"

Frank and I looked at one another while Randy made more agonizing, child-like sounds. We had hardly started this interview, and Randy was becoming an inarticulate mess. We both looked back at the invisible window. Frank took the initiative and dashed out to confer with Daddy and Jennifer. Randy increased his sounds of agony and leaned forward, as if to wretch, then bobbed up again, sucking in air. Frank reentered quietly, knelt beside Randy, who, at this gesture of sympathy, stiffened and looked at both of us in alarm. Frank smiled.

"Don't panic. I'm here to take your order."

Randy's eyes danced in a spasmodic demonstration of disbelief. "You want . . . my . . . order?" he finally managed.

"That's it," Frank said.

Randy blurted out, "Ham and cheese with plenty of mustard on seeded rye."

Frank, "OK, will you take it without seeds?"

"What?"

"If the rye doesn't have seeds . . . ?"

Randy nodded. Frank looked at the window. Randy tried to follow his scrutiny of the impenetrable glass.

"Now relax . . . and maybe we can go on with our conversation till your sandwich arrives. How about that?"

Then Randy moaned one more moan, rose and made a parody of his shackled feet, marching around the room. "I asked to have these taken off. Take them off! I can't eat or speak another word with them on!" In seconds, a guard entered and very swiftly removed the shackles, as Randy stood there looking down at his feet. Once the guard left, Randy shuffled back to his seat, touched his ankles and looked up at Frank and me.

"Where was I?," he asked.

"How long have you worked for Broadway?" I asked as if nothing else had happened. Randy—in a monotone replied, "I've been in the game for like ten years now. And that motherfucker still won't give me a better job. It's like—kind of a slap in the face the way his people treat me. I know it's because I'm white."

Frank added grimly, "You know that the white boy is expendable, right?"

"Until he needs you for something special—but that's been a while now. That bastard stays clear of me because I just run security. He gets his boys to pay me and just assumes I'm too afraid to open my mouth about shit. The last dude, another white boy named Sprig, who had my job got a raw deal. They found him in the river, his hands tied behind his back, all bloated up, floating around by the Bay Bridge last spring. Word was that some psycho strangled one of Broadway's girls in a stash house, lapped her then split. When they found the girl, Sprig didn't or couldn't tell what happened even though he was put on the house as security while they were bagging up."

"Who murdered Sprig?," I asked.

"I heard he's got a squad of killers with all kinds of special ways of turning your lights out for good, in broad daylight, with no remorse. The guy doesn't play games. You need to make sure that me and my family are kept safe when this shit comes down."

"What shit?," I asked. Randy's eyes rolled up in his head, his head sank in his hands and he turned beet red in obvious frustration.

"I know what I'm supposed to do here—SNITCH! On Broadway—but I don't want to go on about that motherfucker right now!"

"Why not? I mean, that's why we're all here," I said.

"Well, I won't 'cause I'm too friggin angry and hungry right at this damn minute, that's why! I just want out of the game and out of Baltimore. Out! Out!

Earlier than anticipated, Jennifer walked into the room and introduced herself to Randy.

"Your sandwich is on its way up," she said soothingly. "Do you gentlemen need a break?," she asked Frank and myself, which meant, "Take a walk". We looked at each other, then at Jennifer. We hadn't even been with Randy fifteen minutes, and we had accomplished zippo—nada—barely broken the ice.

We stepped out into the hallway, Jennifer following. She looked intensely at us and said,

"Congratulations."

"Congratulations for what?," I asked.

"You've got him started at least," she replied.

"Do we come back?," Frank asked, "Or what?"

"That depends," she said, and we heard Randy's voice yelling from inside the room.

"Where's my sandwich?" Jennifer immediately turned the knob, leaving us flat-footed in the hallway. We went directly into the viewing station where Daddy was waiting. His eyes were on Latrell still sitting alone in the other interview room.

"Latrell won't be any easier," he said to us, but before we could say a word, Daddy's telephone rang. He listened, said, "Send it up," then turned to us.

"It looks like maybe a woman's motherly touch is required here," he said, pointing to Jennifer sitting listening to Randy's ongoing babble. "Waste not, want not. We'll take it however we can."

Daddy looked at us, as if to say, "I told you so", a wry smile on his face. Randy had been a ridiculously easy target in the game of self-preservation. A ham sandwich and it was sealed.

Latrell would hardly settle for the same—he had more to lose.

Frank and I left the viewing room and went down the hall. Frank spotted a soda machine on his way in. The excitement of this situation had left us both with dry mouths. Frank bought two Diet Cokes for us. We started toward

Latrell, but Frank stopped in his tracks, went back to the machine and came back with a bottle of fruit punch. Ah yes, I thought—from ham sandwich to fruit punch. But would it work on Latrell with 2 Ls.

Frank and I walked into the room, but, unlike Randy, Latrell stayed in his seated position facing the back wall, not looking at the door to see who walked in. I thought about how interesting that was—he either didn't give a shit who it was, because he'd made his mind up that he was not going to say a word, or he figured that he was going to spill the beans and it really didn't matter who came in to do it. Frank walked in front of me and sat down at the table. He seemed to take the lead on this one right out of the gate.

"What's up, Latrell with two *Ls*? You look thirsty. We got you a fruit drink," and he put it down in front of Latrell, then opened his Diet Coke, taking a long swig, finishing with a carbonated belch.

"So, pal, you know why you're here, don't you?"

Latrell stared back at him, and then turned to the wall with a sneer on his lips. Frank looked suddenly pissed and stood up.

"What the fuck?" He looked at me, sat down and continued calmly, "Listen, let's not waste time. Let's cut to the chase. Latrell! Let me tell you something about you. I know a whole lot about you. I saw the look on your face when you knew we were going to find those bricks in your car. You don't have the balls to carry the weight that's coming down on you. The way I see it, you have only one option—self-preservation."

Latrell kept staring at the wall—a fiercely tight wreck of a man. I felt like it was my cue to jump in.

"Look, Latrell, you think that we don't know who you were running that dope for? Because if you do, you are surely as dumb as you look."

Still staring ahead, he mumbled, "If you know all that, you don't need me, do you?" I was beginning to lose my cool. These two clowns almost seemed to have conspired somehow, to make fools of us so far, and the case was too important. Frank was getting even more fired up.

"That's right, Latrell, we don't fucking need your dumb ass!", he yelled. "But the U.S. Attorney who's going to put you in jail for the rest of your pathetic life made us come in here and give you the courtesy of cooperating. When we leave this room today—whether you cooperate or not—Broadway is done. In fact, you two can talk about it for the next hundred years together . . . if he doesn't kill you first for thinking you ratted him out."

Latrell shook his head, "See, that's some dumb shit I would expect from a Baltimore City po-lice. You bitches come in here—threatening me and shit—and expect me to help you. Shit, man, please!," and he looked at us with a malicious, knowing smile on his lips.

Frank quickly responded, in a softer vein, "That's not a threat, son. That's the way it is. See, you think that you have a leg to stand on here, but you don't have shit. You got nothing but a ten-by-six cell waiting for you. You're having trouble coming to Jesus about what the rest of your life is going to be like as a federal inmate because you have never done time. Those animals are going to turn you out like a two-dollar whore on payday. You don't know what suffering is, because your whole life either the system has paid your way or your pockets were lined with what's left over from Broadway's riches. Don't sit here and tell me that you can handle that shit! You have no idea what kind of hell is in store for your ass. All for what? So you can take it in the ass twice a day and hold your head high because you were a soldier and didn't snitch? Who's going to pat you on the back for not snitching? Latrell, you need to put that childish, corner-boy code horseshit behind you, son, and see this from a different angle. You have a very unique set of circumstances here to change your life path. You're at what I like to call a 'crossroads in life'. The decision to take one road or another has to be made, and whichever road you take you had better be committed to it. And if you don't intend to drink that, I will. It's getting warm."

In a flash, Latrell's arm shot out and knocked the bottle off the table. For a second no-one moved. I could hear the bottle rolling about on the floor, till it met the table legs. Frank calmly stood, picked up the bottle, returned it to its former place and sat down again.

"You're lucky it's plastic," he said. "And it's still cold. You just foamed it up a bit—spread the syrup to make it sweeter on the tongue. I'm going to wait until it's settled down to drink it. Unless, of course, you decide to drink it yourself? Now, where was I? Ah, yes, at the crossroads to a free life—or . . ."

Latrell heard the "free" word and interrupted, "What do you mean 'free'? You can't let me walk on this shit," and he eyed both of us suspiciously.

Frank sat back in his seat and crossed his arms. I took over.

"That depends on you. We don't make the decisions, but, depending on the level of cooperation you give us, who knows? You might be more valuable to us on the street. Shit, you've only been locked up for twenty-four hours. No charges have been filed yet. Nobody knows if you got away or what. If you suddenly resurface with no record of any charges, it would be hard for Broadway to believe the police would let you go carrying that much weight."

Latrell shook his head.

"Latrell, you need to shit or get off the pot on this one, because our window of opportunity to put you back into play is rapidly closing."

Latrell shot a quick look at the soda bottle. He then sat up straighter in his chair and tucked his hands under his thighs, as if to prevent them reaching out for the bottle. The despair on his face was appalling to watch. Frank saw all this and his face took on an ashen look. He turned away and stared at the invisible screen. What he said next could have been addressed to his invisible superiors as well as to the unfortunate man to his left. Frank spoke slowly now, deliberately.

"Latrell with one L or two. I know you want that drink because you're just plain thirsty. Thirsty for what's in that bottle and thirsty for other things. Lots of things. I know the world has not played fairly with people of color. But then, neither has Broadway. He's held you in bondage, son—bondage to his own terror. He's nothing but an urban terrorist. Instead of playing by the rules to make this a better place to live—he's made himself a kingpin to fight this country—and he's gone back to the old slavery times to help him in his fight. Did you ever see yourself in that way? Being a slave to the kingpin's own terror? You heard me—slave. I used that word—slave. You're afraid to drink that soda because you'd be admitting that everything we've said is right. That's how things are going to continue being—taking it up the ass from some prison rat, or taking it up the ass by the kingpin man of color, your color. If you want to keep things that way, then you're right. Don't drink that soda, stay thirsty."

Latrell's hands fell to his sides and gripping the edges of the chair said "What kind of guarantee would I have that I would be taken care of? Broadway's got killers from D.C. to Boston ready to do whatever they're told."

"With your help, we'll pull them all into the case and push for the death penalty," Frank added. "Let me bring you in on a little secret about the feds. You ready for this one? Everybody talks. When you bring in thirty motherfuckers on federal drug charges with the kind of violence that often surrounds their trade, some of them will be looking at capital punishment. You know what that means?"

Latrell mumbled, "Naw."

"It means the needle, death by lethal injection. You put that kind of weight on these dudes, the code goes out the window, and they all start singing to save their own asses. When this thing goes down, all of Broadway's boys will be spilling their guts to stay off death row. It's a fact. Shit, even Broadway will give it up to save his own hide. But if you're willing to do whatever we ask of you to take his organization down, we can talk to the U.S Attorney about what your options are."

Latrell suddenly stood up.

"I need time to think," he said under his breath.

"How much time?," I asked.

"Time, man, time." And unconsciously, he reached out for the fruit punch, quickly opened it and drank down the entire bottle. I had been awed by Frank's tenacity and cleverness but most of all, his humanity.

We looked at one another with the same thought—it was remarkable what one ham sandwich and a bottle of fruit punch can accomplish—even if all the evidence wasn't in on the sandwich side.

When we returned, Daddy was in conversation with Jennifer. He kept us waiting until he was through, then turned to us.

"Well done," he said coldly.

The tireless Jennifer heaved a sigh, "My interview was a bust. Randy kept babbling on about his wife and kids, nothing on the question of the lapping. He was purposefully evasive. Sorry."

Daddy's face hardened, "Guys, that's it for today," then he started to leave. We followed him in single file down to the elevator into the underground garage where Daddy's car was waiting. Jennifer turned and looked back at us, then stepped into the car. Frank and I were left to fend for ourselves.

Later at Hogan's, I remembered Jennifer's last look back at us. "There was a kind of pity in her eyes."

"I caught that too," Frank nodded. "What did it say to you?"

"I felt her pity. And fear. If she's anything more to Daddy than a lawyer, the pity goes both ways." Frank remained silent.

I added, "I'm not sure Latrell will take Daddy's deal—it's too risky—I wouldn't trust a low life like Latrell not to give the whole thing away if confronted by Broadway."

"We'll see," Frank said quietly. "We've come this far. Look, there's got to be some logic in Daddy's head about this."

"Yeah, Daddy may be Daddy, but in the clinch to get what he wants, he may turn out to be no better than the others like him—a heartless fuck." I belched in emphasis. Suddenly, we both laughed and quickly drained our drinks.

Frank in a sincere voice said, "I don't know. Bro—somehow I trust Daddy. Believe it or not, I do. We've both got to trust him—He's the only one I've met with a mission in him."

"What I don't understand is why he hasn't taken action before now. I know what you said, but he's had enough hard evidence . . ."

"Maybe he's had," Frank interrupted, "but for a man in his position, it's still not enough." And he drank the melted ice and liquor residue of his drink in a single gulp.

"It's as if . . . he's been saving his pennies till now . . . to put together what he's really after. Whatever happens will end in a federal court room. Where I'm sure Broadway has even heavier backing and support there than before—the kind of support Daddy is looking out for himself."

"What are you getting at, Bro?"

"There's something beyond his new found moral outrage—the 'good of community' stuff."

I changed my tactics. "How long do you figure Daddy has been in charge of S.I.S?"

"Nine or ten years," Frank said, his worry lines appearing. He went on, "You know, I may sound like a boy scout, but at times like these—trying to keep faith and all. At the moment, I need to believe that Daddy is our avenging angel, OK? That's it, see?"

"Yeah, I see—an avenging angel wearing dark shades."

Frank stared at me. "You know that statue of the Angel of Justice outside the federal court house—She has no eyes to see with—But she's our angel of mercy—of justice—Of vengeance if need be."

I felt a bit of shame in his words, be I understood what he was trying to say and moved on to change the subject.

"Didn't you feel his discomfort later about the slave stuff you confronted Latrell with? It seemed to me he actually resented you talking about that. Didn't you feel it? It looked to me as if he almost resented it. Didn't you feel that?"

Frank said, "I just think it hit him, too."

"Frank, don't get me wrong. I hope he turns out to be just what's needed here. Maybe I do have him all wrong." A long silence followed. We had been fully sobered by our own petard.

"But we did do a pretty decent job back there," I finally said. "Given the circumstances—particularly, you." I leaned across and gave him a clip on the chin.

"Yeah, I guess. But how about that Jennifer broad?" Frank grinned. "With those legs, and the fucking nerve of her."

"She already works for Daddy," I countered. "Whatever way to get what you want? You get it. You heard him. That's what I mean?" There was nothing more to be said.

A short while later, after another round, we left Hogan's—I to meet Marie, and Frank, his latest e-mail catch of the day.

Chapter Eighteen

As soon as I saw Marie, all the bad shit fell off me. We both acknowledged with compelling necessity that, as much as we had missed one another because of our shifts, we still felt like a married couple—even if that fact had not yet been legally sanctioned. She suspected the high-profile move in my career. "Just by looking at you—I can tell." She was wearing one of her dark, form fitting evening dresses—just high enough to turn heads.

"Yes, even if I can't tell you the facts. Sworn not to on oath."

"Oh, I knew that. That's why I knew it was a special assignment. It's written all over you."

"One thing I can tell you—no, two—it means higher pay, and that means . . ."

"You've said it once, don't say it again, Let's save it to savor when—." And she waved at a passing waiter at the restaurant we were at.

"Now hush," she said. I hushed. I always (or almost always) did what she asked.

"Close your eyes." And I did.

"Now open them." And planked down on our table was a bottle of champagne. "It's domestic," she said, "but it's champagne."

"The truth is I wouldn't have known the difference between foreign or domestic."

"Shame on you!"

"Blame my parents," I said forlornly. "They never extended their pallets beyond chardonnay or light merlot."

She poured. We raised and touched one another's glasses. I was feeling suddenly so optimistic about everything. I immediately opted for a refill. Marie put her hand over her glass.

"Not just yet," she said.

"Why not?"

"Because of what you just said."

"About merlot and chardonnay?" But suddenly I understood.

"I couldn't help it. They came into mind." And Marie took her hand off the glass.

"The invisible ones, the unknown?"

"Exactly," she said. "Because part of me wants, would love, if they knew and could be part of it. If you were me, you'd understand."

I looked at her sadly.

"Being a girl, it's all about girlie thoughts. Like my coming up, or is it down, the aisle. I ask myself, whose going to give me away? Don't say it! No, say it . . . Frank, right?"

"Why not Frank?," I protested.

"Oh, I've thought about it. But . . ."

"There's also my father? He'd be a knockout doing it."

"Yes—your father—meanwhile there's still my invisible father."

"Marie, don't do this to yourself. Just consider—your non-existent relationship with that person. You've never even seen him—or her for that matter."

"I know. You're right." She admitted.

But I can't help wishing they could be part of it—of me—of us. I don't even know whom I resemble most—my birth father or mother?"

"Possibly neither one."

"That's mean," she said pointedly.

"Well, look at me! You'd never suspect I was my parents' child. You said it yourself after you met them at that reception. Where was it?"

"The academy. They came to celebrate its 25th anniversary, and I did say that."

"It's true of lots of sons and daughters—and that's a fact!"

"Yes, well you know that and live with it. I don't, and they are still my parents—and that's a fact!"

"Clear my mind of further ignorance. Hasn't Alicia ever clarified anything about them?"

"You always ask that question when the subject comes up."

"And you always offer some . . ."

"That's because I used to ask her—but—well—I've just—I don't know anymore. I'm not sure why, I just don't. Besides, Alicia has enough on her hands—living alone. Minding her little shop."

"Do you think she might be holding back on you—purposely?"

"Yes and no. I've just decided to let well enough alone."

"To brood over, every now and then?"

"Right again." She looked at me, feeling my concern. She smiled and put her hand on mine. "I just keep forgetting visible you when I get this way—don't I?" I merely nodded.

"Alright, okay. I refuse to spoil the rest of the evening, which rightfully belongs to you." She picked up the champagne bottle and poured us a healthy refill. The rest of the evening was an unalloyed joy—which included leaving a mediocre movie to make the most of our bedtime together.

Next morning, we rose early enough to traipse down to our favorite breakfast place, Jimmy's, to meet Frank—a ritual we adhered to depending on the nature of our various shifts. Marie had not seen Frank now for over two weeks and was anxious to congratulate him for his part in our new assignment. A half-hour later, no Frank. I called his cell phone.

Despite his nocturnal pleasures, Frank's stamina was prodigious, and I admired it, knowing where the crack of dawn would find him. I had already left the pleasures of the internet geishas behind me. I called again twenty minutes later—this time I left a message.

Marie pursed her lips. "If he's been where I think he's been, we should let him be. I'm sure you know what I mean."

I smiled my widest.

"I know such habits are hard to break, and someday—you choose it—you must tell me how you managed to abandon yours."

It was a blessed opening to confess. I did so—only surface stuff, but true. "The reason is sitting next to me, waiting to order—and really, Marie, there isn't much to tell once I tell you."

"Johnny, how boring for you!"

"Basically, I was sort of a chaperone for our wayward boy. I'm not wayward by nature." And Marie lifted her eyebrows. "And will never be, I promise you that."

Breakfast finally arrived—silver dollar pancakes, no butter, with blueberry syrup.

"When you catch up with him, hug him for me. Don't imply any knowledge on my part. There's plenty of time to celebrate. In fact, ask him over tonight for dinner." And Marie, on her first day off in weeks, went off to do a bit of shopping, while I high-tailed it to Frank's apartment. There had been no call back on his part yet. Still, I felt something was not right. I knew it. I rang his doorbell—no answer. I parked outside his building for twenty minutes before trying again, this time adding coded taps at the door. Nothing. I called out his name. It was then an elderly lady carrying an empty laundry basket walked by.

She paused at her doorway, which was next to Frank's, and after I rang and knocked again, she said, "He's gone."

I looked at her, in alarm. "Gone?"

"I saw him as I was going down to the laundry room. He left with two men."

"White men or colored?," I asked.

"There was one white and one very large black man. They drove off somewheres."

"Thank you, ma'am," I said and made my way out of the complex. I drove directly to S.I.S., feeling I had been affronted in some way. The squad door opened easily, and I stepped into an empty office. I heard Daddy's voice coming from his office, calling my name."

"Hey, Boss, what's going on?" I asked. Daddy was looking at some file, which he quickly closed. I could only repeat, "What's going on around here?"

"Sit down, son. You look flustered." I sat, and we just looked at one another; but he had intuited the cause of my concern.

"He's gone. I went to his . . ."

"Of course you did," he anticipated me.

"I confess, sir, I felt foolish, and this lady . . ."

"Son, there's nothing to tell . . . yet."

"Yet?"

"Not until the situation stabilizes itself, and we know we can proceed as planned."

"What plan? Sir?"

"Operation White Shadow."

"Is that what it's called? A new name or . . . ?"
"Brand new. Perfect name for it, don't you think?"

"And by 'stabilizing,' you mean just what, sir?"

"That would be saying more than the rules permit me to say."

"OK, so Frank is obviously our undercover man in White Shadow. How do I fit in?"

"I promise you that, as soon as I know, you'll know. Fair?"

"Sir—all fairness aside and with no reflection on Frank—why wasn't I considered?"

"John, you are an officer of an entirely different stripe than Frank Dixon."

"Can you clarify that, sir?"

"Well, let's say you are . . . more refined in appearance and general manner."

"The street thug I've become inside would like to contest that statement."

"That's your own perception and sensibility speaking. The street makes its own distinction—that's part of your effect on the street, even your power. Believe me, all that will be put to good use."

"So, Frank's the apparent thug, and I . . ." I couldn't finish my thought. I just shook my head in disbelief.

"Besides, son, there is one crucial problem why you weren't considered—you don't drive."

"I don't what, sir?"

"Drive . . . a truck. A commercial vehicle." And that was the truthful end to my dilemma.

"We all will have a part in this case. Frank has another assignment that is just as important as yours. You must keep things in perspective when you're dealing with major cases like this. If you don't need to know, don't ask. Trust me when I tell you that if shit goes sideways and word gets out to the wrong people, the fact that you have no knowledge will protect you. I used to work with a Russian detective in Vice who was in high demand for translation after arrests and during search warrants. He used to tell the officers doing the case not to tell him shit about what they were doing, who they were doing or the locations they were going to hit. He believed that, if he was never told the information, when the case specifics got leaked—which they did—they could never point the finger at him. When their cases got compromised, he was the last person to get jammed up. He denied himself the knowledge and took no blame for a corrupt cop who was never identified. You catch my drift?"

Meanwhile, I figured that whatever Daddy put Frank into, I could find out by other means. Daddy was off his rocker about this shit—he was paranoid that everyone was a leak. It is tiresome to always feel that you are being looked at by him as a possible traitor. Something must have happened to him during his career to make him so untrustworthy of fellow officers.

Chapter Nineteen

No matter how I rationalized over the situation, Daddy's choice of Frank as the head honcho in the new operation could not be faulted—but my old devil ego continued batting at me with the smart boy cum laude losing points in the tough world outside where even his looks are against him. If Frank were here at this point, I would both congratulate him and give him a swift kick in the ass. But then I knew he'd grab my face in his hands, look at me until the deepest recognition of who we were to each other showed through—and the hurt would be gone—mostly. I had nothing to do, and with hours ahead before I'd return to the apartment to face Maria with the news, I whiled away the time with the menial of all tasks at S.I.S: wire-tapping logs, the memos of which yielding nothing of real interest, were permanently dumped in the evidence room. One thing was accomplished, the numbing down of my ego's pointless attacks. By the time I made it back to the apartment, I felt in better possession of myself.

The table had already been set for dinner. I could smell some pungent something simmering in the oven. I washed up while Marie rattled on about the perils of shopping for a new outfit while on a pre-fixed budget and her final decision to save money instead. I suddenly realized Marie had set three places at the table. She was wearing one of her best spring numbers, and I automatically said, "Pot roast".

"Frank's showing up isn't he?," She asked. "Don't tell me you forgot to ask him—or what?"

I stood there inhaling the essences of that sweet smelling pot roast, one of Frank's favorites, particularly as prepared by Marie.

"Could I have a glass of wine?," I asked to assuage the sudden tumult in my chest.

"Well, is he or isn't he?" Marie persisted.

"I never caught up with him Marie." I explained the deal as best I could while she poured the wine. I drank slowly. Marie removed her earrings and slowly, filled her glass half way, obviously disappointed at the turn of events.

She stopped drinking and tried to make sense of my scattered story of Frank's new appointment.

"It sounds dangerous to me," she said suddenly.

"What makes you say that?"

"It just does, that's all." And she drank again nervously.

"Danger is part of our business," I said a little sharply. "A fact that you know something about in your own work." I ameliorated.

"There's danger and there's danger—this sounds to me—never mind." She finished her wine and just sat lost in thought, suddenly looking up at me starting her sentence with, "But . . ."

"I said I don't know," I interrupted, "And even if I did, you know I couldn't talk about it, even to you, Marie." The S.I.S code of silence seemed suddenly a convenient excuse for me to not start venting again.

"Well then, what about you, Johnny? Can I ask about you? Did Daddy say anything concerning you?"

"Sure," I added abruptly. "I come down next in line."

"Next in line. I don't like the way you said that," she said anxiously.

"Well, whatever. It's the truth and there's nothing else to say."

"It's just the way you said it—that's all—just Frank and then you, when you join him."

"Who said anything about joining Frank?"

"Well, aren't you?"

"Maybe, maybe not! Please, Marie—let's not go on," and I finished my wine and filled my glass again.

"Just as long as it's not too dangerous," and she rose to go to the stove.

In my head, I said, "Let it be dangerous." The Prince with the Anglo face—me—repeated the thought, wishing it would come true. I wanted to be in the middle of whatever danger was up ahead—with Frank or without Frank. Just there! And I realized and felt a surge of the special tang of danger I'd experienced years ago while hunting deer. I was missing that at this moment . . . missing the rush of excitement—stalking, and killing, the trophy buck. It had been part of my years at college and for a brief time after I joined the force—Frank never became part of that—it had been shoved aside by the immediate needs of the job.

"Well, there will be lots of pot roast left over and a six pack of Buds to wash it down with." Marie said, brusquely, clearing Frank's place at the table. "But Daddy did say you're next?"

I simply nodded, before I added "Only I . . .," and I paused while Marie, Frank's empty plate in her hand, waited for me to complete what I meant to say.

"Only," I repeated, "I'm not sure when the next phase takes place. Okay, no more questions." And I turned toward her still standing by the stove, but not moving.

"Don't you think that might be about done? I'm famished."

Chapter Twenty

In the meantime, before my "assignment" materialized, I was assigned to wiretapping duties and the collating of, to me, undecipherable reports from phone numbers collected from Latrell's cell. My lone-sharkness was exacerbated by Marie leaving to spend time in Connecticut with her ailing mother. This, however, gave me time to carry on my private detective work regarding Frank's whereabouts. I checked his apartment daily, with the same empty results.

By the end of the week, Frank's name was no longer slated on the roster in his apartment's lobby. When I inquired about the apartment, I was told I could take a look at it if I was interested in a rental. I looked around the once-familiar place. It was in the process of having a new coat of paint applied to its two rooms, kitchen and bath. All personal articles—clothing, etc.—had been, you could say, spirited away in the night. To be consigned where? Probably new digs recently acquired. There was no mail in his mailbox and no movement on the telltale tape I'd placed at the bottom of his door. As a last resort, I rode through Pigtown one Sunday, hoping to accidentally run into him. In my addled anxiety about Frank's whereabouts, I'd overlooked one element—Frank, on assignment, would have assumed an undercover identity. Everything about his physical appearance would have changed. I rode back to an empty apartment in a deeply disconsolate state. No Frank. And Marie would not be back for two days.

I was called in to see Daddy the very next morning, his stormy demeanor announced by a hard crack of knuckles before he spoke. "Now that was not a very good idea, son." His stare's single purpose was to unman the man forced to bear its intensity.

"To what are you referring, sir?"

"Brotherly love has its limits, like all love. Your ride through Pigtown was both futile and, in this case, potentially dangerous."

"You had me followed?," I answered in genuine alarm.

He replied with a sharp, "No."

"I was on my own time, sir."

"Nevertheless, this 'Damon and Pithiest' act has to come to an end—as far as this operation is concerned. Your actions force me to reconsider a proposal I was about to make."

I backed off. "What kind of proposal, sir?"

"I've noticed you fidgeting around here—swallowing your pride, chewing your cud. This operation has its carefully calibrated calendar of events. You were not meant to be involved in Phase One."

"You're putting me on the defensive, sir. You know how much I want to be on this team, Frank Dixon notwithstanding."

"Exactly—Frank Dixon notwithstanding. Because Part Two involves you 'notwithstanding' Dixon."

"I understand." I felt like a bona fide asshole.

"Fortunately, your Pigtown visit caused no immediate harm. But it was still ill-considered, particularly after I tell you what it is I have in mind. Now follow me, John. Let me explain how it goes from here."

"Me and Jen have come up with our game plan of how we are going to go after Broadway on multiple fronts. Your part is going to be this: I decided to put you in charge of Fat Randy as his control agent. I want you to use his intelligence on the street to identify Broadway's stash houses and corner crews, then make controlled purchases from them on a routine basis. I will assign an S.I.S team to you as cover and an occasional arrest. This part of the investigation is one of the most important elements in proving our case. All your progress will be documented in house and not on a Baltimore City report. We will keep all the evidence and all the intel gathered from your team's progress in this building. As far as the corner crews and the patrol officers go, you're just a citywide plain-clothes drug unit making an occasional corner bust to boost the stats for the week's command staff briefing. You following me so far?"

"Yeah, I got it so far. Who's going to be on my team?"

"You're going to have J.B. and a few other guys that you haven't met before. They're coming in off other cases to run with this. I want you to use Fat Randy like a two-dollar whore—he owes us huge for keeping his pathetic ass out of federal prison. I want you to make him feel like everything that he is doing is not enough. Keep him hungry."

I understood what he was saying, but interjected, "And for the last time—to satisfy any curiosity—does this new team ever hook up with Frank's unit?"

Daddy looked at me with severe annoyance. "That is not in the plan. Get that straight, John." He then told me to dirty my look up so I could make street-level buys and to come up with a communications plan with Fat Randy. Daddy wanted us to make at least a dozen controlled buys from each crew along with their identifications. The idea was to hang federal conspiracy cases on some of these guys in hope that they would decide to cooperate and agree to testify against Broadway. Agreeing to cooperate—or "proffer," as the U.S. Attorneys called it—provides a free pass on any dirt that they were involved in, even murder. If someone in a proffer tells us that they committed murder for Broadway, they could testify to the fact that they did it for someone else who gets charged with it, but their admission cannot be used against them. A proffer is truly the real get-out-of-jail-free card.

"And I want as much audio-video as possible. Good luck, son."

I left the office feeling humiliated and elated. I was about to do work in Operation White Shadow. The assignment was intriguing and offered new materials for my imagination to play with—but still more secrets to keep. I began to despair about this aspect of my chosen profession. But chosen I had, and I'd continue to make the best of it. And the best of it at the moment was to "dirty myself up".

PIGTOWN

Chapter Twenty-One

Pigtown, U.S.A. is afflicted by a full-blown dope virus. It was the first day of my new assignment. Observing the area through binoculars in a vacant top floor room of a derelict hotel, Pigtown seemed shrouded in a cloud of dust particles. Given the freakish changes in our climate, it could be mistaken for snow heralding an early winter. Its sum and substance is the lingering residue of the drugs imported and exported by Broadway's empire—the source of his power over men, women and, it seems, even children. What lapper could cleanse the sky of his snow?

My team was waiting for me outside the building as I "dirtied" my look up to face the dope corners. Matted greasy hair, dirty jeans with no belt and a t-shirt I fished out of a donation bin at a nearby church, a pair of cracked worn-out black shoes from the same bin, no socks—my disguise. As I looked at myself in a fungused mirror in what was once the grand hotel's lobby, I saw an actor checking his appearance before facing the cameras. A travel-wounded Toyota was on hand to take me to the "set". My team was outside, awaiting its principal player, ready to roll with me into the hub.

I stepped out of the shadows into the hazy sunshine and faced the other players. J.B.—stubble-faced, wearing black baggy shorts and a rumpled Hawaiian shirt—shuffled over to me in his cut-up loafers and signaled to the others. One by one they came forward. No use describing their clothes—they were all "studio" made for the job. The first guy, almost as tall and black as J.B., was staring at me. "How's it goin', golden boy?"

"What?," I said, my first unscripted line.

"That's your nickname," J.B. explained. "Golden Boy, meet 'Ball Buster' from DEA."

"Do I call him that?," I faulted.

"Sure, we all go by nicknames on the street."

The next in line was "Creep" from the FBI. He put out his hand, and I shook it. He was a white man, middle-aged, tall and skinny—matted hair, slack-mouthed with discolored teeth.

Next came "Shooter", our cameraman. Immigration Customs Enforcement or ICE, from Baltimore proper. Not your typical fed, he was in his late 30s, black, fat and hairy.

The next—and I couldn't resist a smile—"The Hulk". The smallest of the group, with a finger-busting handshake. Baltimore City Police all-star, young, tough and obviously street smart.

"What about Fat Randy?", I asked J.B.

"He and Latrell are where they should be," J.B said.

"And you, J.B.? What's your nickname?"

He smiled, "Guess." Nothing came to me.

"Shadow," J.B. said in a whisper.

From what I could see, all were tough and well-seasoned. They had perfected their street personas for years and had adopted the looks and lingos that would fool almost anyone.

When we set off to enter the hub of the neighborhood, all moving in different directions as per our assignments, I was ill-prepared for the holiday atmosphere that greeted us. Corners chock full of worker bees of the dope trade, hawking their wares. Lines of people circling the blocks communicating by eye contact, waiting to get the OK from the dope crew for a quick buy. Young kids rode bicycles up, down, and around this open-air market. Boys on the lookout for the local law's possible intervention. And time and time again, I witnessed the remarkable response to such a situation. It was as if an invisible festive canopy would fold up in the twinkling of an eye. The vendors would disappear from view. The lines of buyers would break up, their need for that fix delayed, while assuming pedestrian attitudes towards one another or merely taking a walk. Once the danger was over—heralded by a sharp whistle from one of the bicycle lookouts—everything resumed, like a pop-up book being reopened. A strange courtesy surged up among these desperate victims, as they resumed their former places in line.

The street vendors formed Broadway's "soldiers", as he called them. His personal army, dressed in uniforms of various kinds—mainly oversized white t-shirts, falling below crotch level against denim trousers or shorts. The young "soldiers" advertised their "specialties" in loud cries that intermingled like some wild yodel or chant—part basis for what became known as "rap" talk. If the caller had a bandana around his neck, that made him the "point" man. A white t-shirt swaddling another's head like a loose turban said ready rock "crack" was at hand. The product was mostly sold in small zip-lock bags or colored top vials. They were always packaged the same—that's how we knew it was Broadway's product. The vials were made of glass and had colored plastic tops, signifying which corners they came from. The crack was cut and measured the same in each vial, like it was packaged at a plant by an assembly line. Sometimes, if we got there in the early morning, the corner crews would put out "testers" to the junkies, which we took advantage of. The dealers would get a small tester package of twenty to thirty pieces of the same coke that was going to be sold there during the day. Tester packages are like a black-market promotional giveaway of free crack, in hopes that the same customers would come back for more later. Although I heard, and part-read my office testimony about these, I had never seen it before and was amazed at how the corner crews would set it up in what they call "the hole". Most times, when they put testers out to the junkies, they would walk out of an alley and throw a bunch of vials in the street. The junkies were like pigeons flocking to a fresh pile of breadcrumbs. I could only imagine the scene.

When it came to quick, high-volume sales, they would set up an area in the hole, with surveillance posts spread out on the rooftops and corners to spot for cops. They would also have young kids acting as junkie wranglers, keeping the masses of addicts in line and out of sight. I even saw a junkie wrangler beat the shit out of some dude who was already so high he couldn't follow directions. I also saw a crew go through a hundred twenty-dollar vials within five minutes. There was a line in the hole and three guys standing side by side, each with a role. One guy took the money, the next guy handed them the product right out of the bag, and the third stood there with a gun in his hand, in case someone decided they wanted to snatch the stash or the money. It was truly barbaric in nature how these people preyed on the weak.

Most astonishing to see was how young these purveyors of solace were—kids from twelve, fifteen, seventeen. Babies looking at you sideways, as their deft fingers handled the merchandise. These corner crews would make CIA counter-surveillance teams look veritably like schoolchildren. The kids had learned the heartbeat of the streets to the point they were able to pick out what fits and what doesn't.

Early on, I was served a resounding lesson in the department of "fitting in". I waited my turn on a dope line, but this kid—maybe sixteen or so—had his eye on me. He kept looking back at me like he recognized me from someplace. Before he sent his runner out to get my order from a ground stash, he asked me to show him the soles of my shoes. He took one look and told me, "We're not selling here, cop." I walked away and played it off like a pissed-off junkie, but nevertheless absolutely floored that this kid was able to spot a cop based on the soles of his shoes. I was later schooled by J.B. that the soles of a junkie's shoes need to be worn and beaten on, as if they had walked miles through a crack-vile-filled alley. I guess the dealer looked at the bottom of my shoes and didn't see the wear and tear of a junkie, which only added to his primal street sense of me being the law dog. He could probably smell the fear coming from me.

I later changed my footwear and bought from the same kid who saw so many junkies each day he forgot about me.

I was still a rookie at this point. I was told that the hardest thing about working undercover is being able to act natural. If you're the slightest bit unsure of your actions, your cover is blown. If too nervous or too aware, you're busted. At this point, the Academy Award had eluded me. Once I understood such tactics, I became daily alert as to where to go. Very quickly, I learned which crew felt comfortable selling to me. The ones that didn't, we just sent another member of our team in. The "Hulk" was our prize substitute and the best actor on the set. Soon we were making roughly ten to fifteen purchases a day, spending upwards of fifty dollars a buy.

Meanwhile, Fat Randy was in his element. He would send me text messages when the drug crews were up and running and give me the street name, along with descriptions of who was involved and where their ground stashes were located. These crews would very seldom keep the vials on them; instead, they would find a good hiding place that was easy to get to and hidden from anyone watching them from the street. They would put the bag of vials in the hiding spot and only go to it when a sale was being made. Alleyways, vehicle gas tanks, trash inside of trashcans were all common hiding places. Before going to make a buy, our surveillance "shooter" would try to creep into the area and get set up for some video coverage of the sales.

There was another pair of eyes watching as I moved from line to line. I had avoided him, because he seemed the oldest of the "soldiers", with more "experience" behind him than the others. I feared he would one day point a finger at me and completely reveal me for the hoax I was. His name was "Peanut", another nickname of course. In size and attitude, he was anything but. Tattoos seemed to be sprouting out of his shirt—names and more names, flowers, serpents, and crosses. A plain looker with large ears, he was a walking cornucopia of the art. I thought of Frank and his lady of choice, Marjorie Wyatt, an art gallery herself.

I dropped my guard to look around at where I was. Who knows? Frank might be watching me from some window. I felt a hand on my arm and turned to face a somber face. The jig was up, and then came the smile—a broken front tooth of a smile, but a smile nonetheless. Peanut had broken into my reverie, which may have looked like an addict's trance to him. I purchased my vials.

Peanut rapidly became my preferred dealer. Curiously, I felt safe around him—which was hard to explain. His chant had a benevolent edge to it, strange to say. It signaled a smooth sell to hell and back. Had Lourdes a malevolent adjunct to it, and was Peanut the keeper of its flame? His voice was gentle, in sharp contrast to his occupation.

One detail I was forced to live with—my veteran Toyota, the only vehicle to be parked daily in the hood I was working. Cars came and went, equally feeble in appearance with their drivers to match. They were peripatetic junkies, while I was practically in residence. As such, my only vehicle became a source of curiosity among the panhandlers of bliss. One young boy in particular kept coming back to it, as if it were some special museum piece on display. He was one of the "bicycle lookouts", who were sentinels against police invasions. He was also a purveyor of the vials from one street to another. This boy couldn't be more than fifteen and, in appearance, was flamboyantly different from the rest of the corner crews. He was light skinned, his hair a mass of curls wreathing an imposing head. He was muscularly thin, lithe and exotically handsome in his way. I saw him walking round and round the Toyota—touching its surfaces, peering through its windows. Fortunately, I kept it locked and windows shut, despite the heat of the day. There was nothing really to observe. The one object that would have interested him was hidden away in a small compartment up front—a glock.40-calibre handgun I kept for security. I never wandered too far from the car and kept it always in sight while playing my role.

The boy usually lingered round the car for minutes at a time, then would blithely hop back on his bicycle to resume his rounds. But one day, I caught him trying to get into the Toyota—surreptitiously looking around while tugging at the door on the driver's side. I walked ever so in character towards him and watched him at his futile labor. He saw me, figured who I was, and, with a slight smile, said, "This your car, mister? I think maybe it is. Peanut says it is, too." His English was clear, but tinged with some accent I couldn't immediately place.

"Yes, it's my car," I said, maintaining my veiled addict voice.

"Abu-man promise me a car for my next birthday, when I come to sixteen." He grinned, not showing teeth.

"Abu-man?," I asked.

"Yeah! Top father, Big Boss. Abu-Broadway." He pronounced it "Boardway".

"Can I be of help?," I suggested.

"Yeah, I don't know that thing you got in back." I looked to where he pointed in the car.

"Do you mean my rosary?"

"Ros-ary, yeah."

"What about it?"

"It look like it got no power in it," he said. "What for you got such a thing? My gamma, she got one long one with black beads that big around. She beats me with it sometime—it has power in it. It never breaks."

"It's not to beat anyone with," I softened. "It's a good luck charm."

The boy nodded, as if he understood. "You mean magic charm?"

"Something like that."

"What's your name, mister?" His fifteen-year-old voice momentarily cracked.

"Ah, ah . . . Johnny. And your name?," I ventured.

"Kalique." And he actually spelled it out for me. "But I'm called 'Wings.'"

"'Wings'? Ah . . ."

"Because of my bicycle. I am the fastest one of all. 'Wings,' see?" Then his black eyes went back to the rosary.

"You're not from around here?," I asked carefully.

"No one is. Abu bring us together. He bought me from my village in Morocco."

"He bought you?"

"And my gamma—same price. Kafir from the same place, too. My cousin."

"Kafir? Who is . . . ?"

"Him. Peanut." And he laughed, sounding even younger than he was. "Kafir . . . Peanut here before I came."

I heard this cry from one of the vendors, "Kalique, you come here now!" It was Peanut himself, shouting in our direction.

"I'm doing business, Kafir!" he yelled in response, then turned back to me. "Soon I be back to sell in my old job. We take turns in everything. You'll buy from me then, mister?"

"Come! Quick!," Peanut shouted again. "Broadway's car just coming in. Come here, you little fuck!"

Kalique merely relaxed and leaned against the Toyota. "Abu is coming to check in," he said. For some reason, I flushed and fumbled for my car keys. Kalique straightened up and moved to make more room for me. I let the car's rancid air out and left the door opened. Kalique's face brightened.

"You can look inside if you like," I said. And he did, sticking his head inside the Toyota like a turtle coming out of its shell.

Peanut's voice rose in sharp command. "Kalique, you hear me, boy?" And the turtle head returned to its shell. The boy walked past the headlights and yelled, "Kafir, I'm coming!" And without another word, Wings slowly ambled back to where Peanut stood awaiting him.

I slid into the car, shut the door and turned on the less-than-efficient air conditioner. From this vantage point, I could observe the great man's entrance with impunity.

"Broadway" arrived in a tinted-out black Ford Expedition. He parked by a large, gray sofa that had been eviscerated and dumped to grace a street corner. As the car appeared, children and adults entered from various side streets, as if from some cue on a movie set. The vendors came forward in measured steps, like an honor guard. Their hands were raised in salutation and a salute. It was my first sight of Broadway, aside from photos. A huge, black, silk suit emerged from the backseat. His ruby-fingered right hand preceded him, already in play. Lightly, his stubby fingers moved in a kind of—yes—blessing. The gathered mob closed in on him—children bouncing up and down on the destroyed sofa, waving skinny arms and yelling, "Abu! Abu!" The cry was picked up by the older worshippers, reaching out to touch their god, although none actually touched him. They were almost zombie-like in their adoration. I had already seen their dead eyes, which occasionally flashed in bodies that hadn't caught up with their true conditions.

Abu moved forward, and the crowd opened up before him. Grandly, he approached his "soldiers", waiting on the periphery to offer their homage. As palms met palms in greeting, I wondered how many had been bought and brought in from distant countries. Who were the agents collecting them for Abu's little army?

As Broadway reached Peanut and Kalique, he pressed his left hand against Peanut's head and, with his right, grabbed Kalique by his curls and pulled him into an embrace. "Prince" should have been Kalique's nickname, from this evidence. And the "Prince", patting the fat man's shoulders, took it all as if it was his due.

I was in another world. I felt I was watching a documentary of life lived somewhere other than in the confines of Pigtown, U.S.A.

Suddenly, Abu's arms left Kalique's smaller frame. He looked over the assembled crowd, many of whom were sitting on the curb, and I could swear I saw him sniff the air. A quick change came over him. He turned around abruptly and, in small steps, marched nervously back to his car. I could imagine the kingpin's thoughts. "Don't stay too long, Abu-way. You never know who's mingling in the crowd." The uniformed chauffeur maneuvered the Expedition as best he could through the crowd, whose leechlike fingers held onto it, forcing the driver to be wary.

The car was gone, and abruptly everything returned to normal—the crowd to where they'd come from, the vendors to their afternoon customers. It was as if the visitation hadn't occurred. Kalique ran back to my Toyota to pick up his bicycle, resting against the wall of a nearby house. He tapped the window of my car, and I lowered it.

"Remember, you promised to buy from me. I will look for you." And with another glance at the rosary, he smiled and said proudly, "That's your charm . . . to buy from Kalique." And in a swift move, he hopped on his bike and made off to his station.

It was the same for us, when the team reunited before sundown.

Chapter Twenty-Two

. . . .

One of our top priorities was to identify where the stash houses and cooking houses were located. This was where Fat Randy earned his keep. They pulled him off the security detail for the packages coming in and put him as a lookout in the alleyways and corners near the houses. Randy very often was not even in the area when the cocaine made its way into the houses, but sometimes he was able to get tag numbers of drop vehicles. The most important part was that he could identify which houses were being used. They made it hard to conduct surveillance on the houses by constantly switching locations. Most of all, because of the women recently being murdered, lapping had been forbidden.

The way these stash houses were created is the definition of the word "ingenuity" itself. The majority of the houses were owned by the same entity. I did some digging on at least two dozen houses that Broadway's people used to get their dope street-ready and found the owner of the property to be listed as a small business called "B&B, Inc." The company gave a post-office box as its address and had a phone number with just an answering machine and an electronic voice message. We later found that this business was set up by Broadway's people as a minority-owned community rehabilitation front. The company would get a minority preference from city hall to sell abandoned city property for a dollar. They would rehab the house to make it livable and supposedly rent or sell it to someone who would pay taxes and improve the neighborhood. The reality of it was that Broadway would use the house to cut up and stash his drugs, then claim the rent money as profit, therefore paying himself and laundering his drug money. The house would be set up with an electric and phone account in someone else's name, just in case the city decided to check on his revitalization efforts. I bet that if we dug deep enough, we would find direct ties to the corrupt politicians at city hall who chose his company to give the properties to. I'm sure that the Mayor or City Council person in that district got some campaign contribution checks with the title "B&B, Inc." on them. This kind of shit is exactly what this city is made up of. Nothing is what it appears to be, and the corruption runs from the streets up to the Mayor's office.

Daddy was constantly asking for intel on the lapping—whether it was dead or what. He asked me to push Randy back into the fetish market with Broadway and get the lapping parties back in business.

And one day, I brought it up, "Randy is there any way you could get your old job back?"

"I don't know if I want it back!"

"You had a good record with Broadway. If you could persuade him to take you on again, it'll win big points for you when this goes to court."

Randy heaved a sigh, quickly mulling the possibilities and advantages of such a move. "It'll take time," he repeated.

"We're not off this case till it's time to go. I'll let Daddy know you're thinking about it, OK?"

"OK, you do that," Randy said, half-resigned to the proposition.

Preservation of life at all costs. Who knows, if Randy succeeds in his assignment, we might still get our footage after all. The irony of this hit me forcibly. Here I was in a covert operation, needing to protect that position, while giving orders to a lowlife with invisible handcuffs on him—all adding more clubs to the juggling act I was involved in.

I'd made every attempt I could to get back to S.I.S every night to file my daily reports and shed my disguise before getting back to Marie. But more and more interferences popped up. There were late night drug deliveries to various stash houses, forcing us to remain on tap for the necessary film we needed to establish this fact. On occasion, one of the team (including J.B.) had to help me at S.I.S with the reports. On these evenings, I found myself either sleeping in my Toyota on my old post midnight shift sleeping hole, or, unable to bear the dank carryover of my daily hygiene, I'd take a room in some sleazy motel for the night that had a shower. My calls to Marie, always in danger of being intercepted from either side, became more sporadic. The nights I did manage to get to the apartment became tense with my inability to say anything about myself or my daily activities. It became variations of "how was your day" ending with Marie going on with her own merciless routines at the hospital, ending in prolonged silences and exhaustion. Both claimed and dimly saved us in each other's eyes. Love making was practically non-existent. Several attempts to assuage proved futile and ultimately embarrassing.

One night, I woke up to find Marie searching my clothes, smelling my shirt, my trousers even for some tell-tale deception each article might reveal. It was on that night that Marie asked, "How's Frank?" I lay there in bed, unwilling to go where she was trying to lead me.

"I asked you a question, John," she said with suppressed hostility.

"I'm still wondering about that myself," trying to remain as calm as I could manage. "I've been looking everywhere for him. I'm beginning to think his assignment has taken him somewhere else. I shouldn't even be telling you this—you know I shouldn't."

She dumped my clothes on to the floor in response. I sat up, slowly but deliberately. Somehow Marie, mistaking my intentions, ran and locked herself in the bathroom. I followed and spoke to her from my side.

"Marie, don't make it any harder than it is! If I knew about him, I'd . . ."

"What if you knew?" she answered in a tight, abrasive voice. "You'd tell me. Right? Wrong!"

"I think you'd better come to bed. You're on a day shift starting tomorrow."

"Don't tell me what to do or not to do. You know what I think? What I really think, Mr. S.I.S? You know exactly where Frank is in your Pigtown rendezvous."

"Sure!," I yelled back. "Of course, we meet every night in some undercover house and share a new crop of internet whores. And let me tell you, they are beauts!"

"Don't you ridicule me—you liar—don't you dare! I'm sick of you . . .," and on and on till ultimately one of us ended up on the couch—usually me—to get a measure of sleep we both needed to face the next excruciating day. Little by little, a freeze began to develop between us—making things even more intolerable. Yet we still loved each other—I never gave up on that—and hopefully—despite everything—neither did Marie.

I'd been leading this life since June and here it was, a week into August. Out of it with Marie, no news from Randy and my nerves beginning to unravel. I felt desperate. I must have looked desperate. Perfect in fact for my job—but not my soul.

I thought of Frank—looked for him all over town with no results. I was beginning to give up on ever locating him.

Chapter Twenty-Three

I got back to Pigtown at eight the next morning, after my sharp exchange with Marie, wearing dark sunglasses to hide the bags under my eyes. I greeted each of the team in a daze and waited till noon to get on Peanut's corner. There would be a small break for lunch, delivered by various denizens of the side streets—mothers, very young girls or boys, related to the vendors or not. They would bring fast food and drinks. The reward? A small vial to do whatever they chose to do with it. Invariably, it was to either use it themselves or sell it in saved candy wrappers. Indeed, it was a thriving community. The junkies waiting for lunch break to be over or the police to clear the area would sit on curbs, some holding their knees with their heads on top, in obvious pain to get a fix.

Peanut was already chewing on what looked to be some kind of meat—fried chicken?—sandwich laced with a thin coating of lard. The fare often consisted of grain cakes or plantains and other cut-up fruit bits. The break was also the occasion for chats between Peanut and myself if he was in the mood. Chewing hungrily on his sandwich, he started the conversation in his amiable, even courtly manner peppered with roughhouse.

"I hope my little cousin didn't bust your balls too bad. He likes cars and things that move fast. He's fifteen. What can I say?"

"I understand," I said. Not having had any breakfast that morning, I was still squeamish at what he was shoveling into himself. It must have translated as another kind of hunger on my part.

"I don't see your cousin around this morning," I said.

Peanut bit a large chunk out of his sandwich. He waited until he had control of it in his mouth before answering. "He'll be working a couple of blocks away. It'll be his first day back selling." He eyed me closely as he chewed. "Don't worry, he's just like that. Makes people promise to do things for him. The next day, he forgets who and what it was."

"Yeah, he did make me promise I'd buy from him."

"Did you say you would?"

"Naw!"

"There, you see what I mean?," and finished his sandwich.

"Are you sure he won't hold it against me?," I edged on.

"Don't worry. But if he should, just say you'll think about it and tell me."

"I don't want to cause any trouble," I edged. (And I meant that to forestall real trouble.)

"I'll talk to him," Peanut reassured. "He's done this before. Every now and then, he remembers, but he has a small business head."

"I'll take you at your word. I don't want to hurt his feelings."

"I said I would take care of it. You're my customer."

He nodded to himself, then took out an ivory toothpick from his vest pocket, and began to work his mouth. He worked slowly, delicately, as if imitating someone he'd observed.

I quickly changed the subject. "I heard something about a psycho killing one of the girls working here in the neighborhood."

He then put a hand up to cover his mouth as he spit out residual bits of his lunch. He wiped the toothpick on his trousers and replaced it in his vest pocket.

I watched all this a short distance away-sitting on the curb taking a junkie siesta.

"Well," I ambled on. "I just hope they catch the guy that did it."

"They never do," he said with candor. "But if the girl was alive, she'd appreciate what you just said."

"Did you know her?"

"No. I like to love straight, if you get my meaning." And he bumped his pelvis in explanation.

I nodded three small times and thought, "Does a tongue leave a tongue print?" Then I said, "Somebody must have known who he was."

"Cops around here? They don't give a fuck!" And with a wave of his hand, he blew them away. "I mean, they make a little noise about it," he added, "but the next day, it's as if it never happened."

"How's that?," I insisted.

"It's part of the whole package, man. This time I made sure I wasn't hit for any stash."

"You mean they get . . . ?"

"A payoff! Sure, what do you think? Nobody worries much about it, and Abu makes sure we get our dues back, in case we're hit for it."

"Do you take any . . . ?"

"Sometimes, for kicks. Look around you. Some of their fingers don't know what they're doing—like picking at candy. It gets a lot of them hooked before they know it. But as I said, I never get hooked. And I never will, particularly now that I'm retiring."

"Retiring? You're retiring?"

"Yeah, it's great, isn't it? I'm seventeen years old, and I'm retiring."

"At your age? How is that possible?" I was confused at the thought. "How long have you been in the game?"

"Since I was fourteen, but I'm not talking money. 'Retiring,' for many of us, has a different meaning to it."

"Such as?"

Peanut lost his smile and looked at me with sudden suspicion.

108

"I'm sorry," I said. "Am I asking too many personal questions?"

He scratched his head, then very simply said, "Would you do me a favor?"

"If I can."

He took a pause and smacked his lips together several times. "Would you show me the bottom of your shoes?"

And we were back there, but "back there" has been months past when it was first asked. "Why?," I asked with perfect ingenuousness mixed with fatigue.

"Just do it."

I shrugged and lifted first my right foot and then my left. I noticed that Peanut's associate was watching.

"I thought so, but you've got to be careful, man."

"Careful?" I'd worked very hard to overcome that flaw of the sole. "You took me for a cop?" It was my best moment so far. I'd asked that same question of myself recently.

"It never hurts to check." There was a stillness now between us as he explained. "Man, listen, they come here—the big city cops—the 'knockers' who get sent here to wreck our business."

"I'm sorry to disappoint you then," and continued my performance of being affronted.

"Look, I'm sorry, too, but what the hell? I've never run into one yet, but when I do . . . !" He bit his hand and made a chopping gesture with it.

I became aware that the line was beginning to form again. The lunch break was over.

"But don't you worry about my cousin," he said in a conciliatory manner. "He'll do what I tell him."

I said, "Thanks," and walked away.

I had passed the test on the second go-around. I felt like I'd graduated from rookie to who I really thought I was. I went back to my Toyota a few blocks away, aired it out, then sat inside, reviewing my conversation with Peanut. Almost all the other vendors were basically suspicious and truculent, except for the two cousins. Kalique was solicitous for business purposes; Peanut already had my business. And yet I felt now that he was also being solicitous, answering my questions as he did. Who was leading who on? To where? Or was his solicitousness another way of ferreting out the enemy? I checked my shoes. The soles had been carefully honed, and yet . . . ? Then there was this mysterious "retiring" gambit, where his willingness to explain had taken a backseat. It had been the first hitch in our "negotiation". I knew I would have to be extra cautious in my dealings with him from now on.

Next day, members of our squad were making their usual controlled purchases from a couple of corner crews in the Westport area. I held back, purposely avoiding Peanut's corner till another day. I rode around in my uneasy frame of mind, with my .40-calibre handgun concealed between the driver's seat and cup holders in case something went wrong.

Ten blocks away, I circled an area where I spotted Kalique chanting the name of the daily product. I don't know if he spotted my car or not, but I hurtled out of there.

I was on the lookout for Randy again, with news that he had managed to make contact with the big boss. It had been two weeks since our conversation, but alarmingly there was no Randy to be found. I decided to chance it with Peanut—rationalizing that my appearance on the day following our "little chat" would auger well for me.

I pulled through the area, anticipating seeing Peanut in his usual place. Instead, it looked like a whole new crew was in place. They were positioned in the familiar spots and wore the standard white t-shirts and black shorts or denims that everyone else wore. I drove through slowly and made eye contact with the corner "boss", who waved me over. In all the time I'd been in Pigtown, such a shift had never taken place till this moment. Why now?

I decided to keep going and would loop the block as if I was being cautious. As I pulled away, I looked in my side-view mirror and saw this new corner boy whistle to another one of his workers and make some signal with his hands that I didn't recognize. This whole thing was messing with my cop senses, like they were planning to rob me or take my car. Ignoring my best judgment, I looped the block and came back through using a side street. When I pulled up to the corner, I suddenly got chills and the hair on the back of my neck started standing up. Just as I was trying to get my hand on my weapon, the young boy who had whistled came out of the alleyway, pointing a sawed-off, single-barrel shotgun at me.

I looked up at him, and everything just went into slow motion. I could see straight down the barrel, and the sight of the gun consumed everything as it was pointed at me. Instinct and the will to survive kicked in. I hunched down in my seat and jammed my foot on the gas as the boy's shotgun went off, blowing out my backseat window and spraying glass throughout the interior of my car.

Head down, I continued through the intersection and turned the next corner to park near the alley. I was hoping that the surveillance teams were already out of their hiding spots and on his ass. I fumbled to get my gun from between the seats and, while doing so, fired a shot through my floorboards, nearly missing my own foot. I was so hopped up on adrenalin that the report from the shot sounded like a cap gun. I jumped out of the car and ran to a parked car at the other end of the alley. I looked around quickly—no local cops even remotely in sight. I moved to the back of the car, using it as cover to get a better angle on the corner where the shooter first assaulted me. Just as the corner came into view, the short barrel of the shotgun telegraphed the little shithead coming at me. He must have thought that the first shot wounded me and that, with a follow-up, he could finish me off. I kept unconsciously seeing the image of his twelve-gauge shotgun shell next to my tiny .40-calibre round and felt inadequate in this fight. I was outgunned and, being bottlenecked in between two buildings and a car, in a terrible position to defend myself. My heart was pounding so furiously in my chest that I couldn't talk or yell for help. I was accepting the fact that I was probably going to be shot.

As the rest of the gunman came around the corner, he saw me duck behind the rear tire. He cranked off a second round in my direction that blew out the back window of the car I was using for cover. I crouched down and absorbed the deafening sound of his shotgun and heard the sound of him breaking the breach to chamber another round. The glass from the back window tricked over my head and through my hair. I fell on my ass, facing the back of the car, and raised my gun up in expectation that he would come around that corner into my field of fire. Instead, I heard a short series of close-range pops that were the familiar sound of a .40-calibre handgun, then silence. I remained sitting behind the car for what felt like an eternity, afraid to pick my head up to see what was going on. I looked at my hands-they were shaking out of control. God knows how long it was until I heard the familiar voices of my S.I.S cover team running up to me. I figured that hearing their voices meant that they had shot the suspect in the back before he got to me. I peeked my head above the buckshot-splattered trunk to see the killer lying face down, gun still in hand and a large chunk of his skull and brain spilling out of the side of his head. The S.I.S crew came running up to me with their guns drawn, looking around furiously.

"Oh my god, are you shot?" I still couldn't believe what had just happened. I was in such shock that I couldn't answer the question, other than to say, "I don't know." Creep holstered his weapon and ran over to me, pulling my shirt up, looking for bullet holes. I became panicked that, if shot, I'd feel nothing. Creep pulled half my clothes off and blurted out to the rest of the team that I was OK. I looked at the body on the ground and was glad that he was dead. I felt absolutely no remorse and no feeling whatsoever for this kid. I looked up at the team, all of whom were staring at him on the ground. Creep put his arm around me, "Golden Boy, you lucky son of a bitch, you got him with a head shot. It saved your lily-white ass."

I looked up at him and realized that he thought I shot this kid. "Creep, I didn't shoot this kid. I thought you guys did."

Creep was one of those guys who didn't rattle that easily. "Son, before we got to you, we heard like three pops from your forty. When we got through the alley, we found him like this. There's no other explanation."

And yet I knew there was one. As I tried to get my bearings, part of the explanation presented itself. The kid who had attempted to take my life was one of Peanut's runners known as Monkey.

As the distant sounds of responding police and med units broke the silence, Creep ordered everyone to quickly abandon the scene and meet back at S.I.S.

COUNT THE GAINS; TOSS THE LOSSES

Chapter Twenty-Four

The next day, I was back at S.I.S permanently, my Pigtown assignment terminated.

"I can't afford to lose as able an officer as you, John. You're not going back to Pigtown. That action on you was no accident. I know the Piggtonians well enough to read the signs. Besides, you've amassed an incredible amount of viable evidence to start putting our case into motion. Congratulations to you and your team." And Daddy patted me on my back.

These were the first words of praise I'd heard for months, five and a half months—I had lived and breathed Pigtown shit. The pigeon shit outside S.I.S was now Chanel in comparison.

Yes, I'd been around street shootings before, but never had I come so close to being the victim. The details of that attack kept pursuing me as much as Frank's Iraqi nightmares pursued him. I had pushed my luck too far, certainly with Peanut. Who else but Peanut had put the finger on me? Deception on deception. I even entertained another scenario, unwilling to give up on Peanut entirely—namely that, for whatever reason, he had reversed himself and been my last-minute savior. If so, why? Things had moved with lightning speed after our little lunchtime chat, but surely Peanut was in no position to mastermind the complete shift of the dope corners that crucial day. Or had Randy, in my search for him, decided to become a turncoat? However one looked at it, the big maneuver against me had been orchestrated by Broadway. No other authority could have managed to warn the local cops away from the shootout.

I thought of Frank, still slogging in the entrails of the Pigpen, and the possibility of him being an imminent target, if my conjecture on Randy's betrayal held water. My mind kept twisting this way and that, in this web of conspiracy enveloping me. Daddy agreed that, in the final stretch, Broadway took over. But as to pointing a direct finger at the informant behind the action, Daddy remained as uncertain as I.

The team remained on course to continue their activities. Automatically, this news exonerated Randy from culpability. In the final analysis, the team had arrived at the penultimate moment, still insisting that, despite my disclaimer, I'd personally won the battle with my glock. J.B., with Creep's help, had bagged any personal items of mine left in the pulverized Toyota, then left the vehicle to be dealt with by the locals when they finally and futilely arrived. The bag showed up two days later with J.B.'s report on the events during and pursuant to the attack. J.B.'s report indicated that things had just gone on as usual—or, in Pigtown parlance, "it was just another dead yo boy." J.B. had reported that there was no possible way he could obtain info about the absence of the local police in the attack. To attempt to do so could blow the whole operation. A "P.S." on his report indicated that the Pigtown police saw to it that the two vehicles had been removed and the street cleaned of glass shards and blood stains.

As to my personal items, I was ready to consign them to the trash when it hit me—the rosary was missing. I went over the items again. No rosary. Had Kalique made off with it during the confusion? He was working blocks away when the shooting started—either that alerted his attention or he was in on its inception. He must have seen me that day driving through his area, and my not stopping might have incited him to act. Another scenario offered itself—and a mad one, to boot? Did some local officer pocket the rosary? I was fixated on this fact. It all circled back to Kalique and his curious interest in it. I determined it was in his possession, whether he colluded with Peanut or not in betraying me.

A frustrating silence fell over the event, and J.B.'s reports thereafter shed no further light on the matter. I'd returned to the apartment the night the incident took place. I attempted to remain as calm as I could. After all, I had survived.

That night I woke up screaming, spewing out disconnected words. My dream world had been invaded by what I'd gone through. I saw an image of myself—a faceless one facing a barrage of shattered glass. Marie held my sweating body in her arms until I quieted down. By morning, after a hot bath and a light breakfast, I felt in better shape. I broke cover. I owed it to Marie, and I told her what had happened in Pigtown. Her dark intuition on the danger that might overtake me had taken shape. As I spoke, I felt as if I were describing another man—another John Larkin. For the rest of the week, my beautiful Marie became my nurse, spooning out her love and any chicken soup remedy at hand. I reported my condition to Daddy, who listened silently. By the end of the week, I was expected to return to S.I.S. There was work to be done, to finish collating the reports and evidence I collected for the upcoming grand jury presentation.

"Every bit of intel and evidence will be categorized so you can begin assembling it into some coherent shape," were Daddy's final words before he hung up.

Back at S.I.S, I did not inquire about Frank and his contribution to the case. That same night during dinner at the apartment, Marie and I closed the gap that had widened between us—offering mutual apologies for our intransigencies toward one another during the Pigtown assignment. "It's been the first big rift we've had, and the sooner we put it behind us, the better. Don't you agree?"

Marie hesitated before nodding. But that hesitation spoke volumes. I felt she was holding something back. She was biding her time for some reason, and I did not push her any further. I intuited what was on her mind, growing into determination all during her ministrations to my, let's face it, break-down. We had by now been dining at home regularly since, and finally I spared her the burden of having to put it into words. We had just finished dessert, a chocolate cake from our local pastry shop.

"Marie, I understand your concern but, I can't. The thought of quitting has passed through my mind, too. But as I just said, it passed. I know you've been thinking about this, waiting to find the right moment to speak your mind. It's the chance one takes—given the profession—some never get to that point. Some do. I did, and I'm sitting here opposite you now. What's out there is still out there, and it's still got to be dealt with. It's become too deep a part of me," and I reached over and took her hand, leading her to the couch before I continued.

"For years, my parents tried to dissuade me from becoming what I am, a cop. They felt it a demeaning, blue collar kind of work. My father is still determined, so he obsesses about my taking over the family business, Larkin Associates. The finest in men's apparel. He dreams of seeing in his lifetime the Associates, turned into Larkin and Son. If that is in the cards somewhere down the line—so be it. My father is an industrious, vigorous man, who, at 68, still attends to his job as manager and proprietor. The idea of retiring hardly crosses his mind. Oddly, what I'm saying to you I could never say to him. It would perplex and confuse him and his sense of values, for I would be using words like destiny and love for my work. It's not just a duty job, needing someone to do it. It's a loving need to bring some order to a disordered world. Frank feels the same way. We know being a police officer can be a rotten, often degrading business, but our intentions are still honorable, and until proven otherwise, destiny has put us on its path to do what we can to help. It brought you to me. You're in my blood now, and that makes up for everything. This incident in Pigtown can't blot all that out. I'd be a coward if I gave into it. I'd be a coward to the deepest part of me. So trust me. I think you understand. I think you always have. In its own way, the work you do at the hospital represents that same need. To help. To say, goodness still exists and is still possible."

Marie said nothing for a long while. She went about with her coffee fixings. When she came back, there were tears in her eyes. She sat down next to me, let her tears flow and said, "Just don't die on me, Johnny. Don't."

"I won't."

"Promise me," she insisted, as if saying so would convince the powers of the universe.

"I promise," and I put my arms around her and pressed her gently against me.

THE PARTY

Chapter Twenty-Five

The moment I picked up the phone in the apartment, I knew I was in for it. My father's voice was fraught with anxiety. Tears signaled my mother on her extension. Still on their summer vacation in Maine, they had finally managed to corner their errant son. It was a long conversation, mostly spent in my disabusing them that all was not right with me in Baltimore.

"We actually thought you'd been killed," Mother kept repeating.

"I can tell you, not knowing young man," my father interjected, "has put a pall over our stay here this summer."

"I was on a particularly demanding assignment, Dad."

"So demanding you couldn't call just to say hello? You've shown unprecedented negligence. It's not pleasant being the butt-end of my only son's growing indifference," etc., etc. Indifferent? No. But they were right—and still there was no help for it.

"I'm sure your lady friend had more cognition of your whereabouts than us," etc., etc., etc. Then both started in again on my chosen profession.

I just listened and offered my profuse apologies, along with a promise to make it up to them in future. Getting older, they were becoming less stoic about my way of life. They settled down finally, and I did manage to get Dad back on his favorite pastime, golf.

I'd hardly hung up when the phone rang again. I picked it up immediately, against my wishes. As usual, I assumed Mother had forgotten to tell me something. Instead, I recognized J.B.'s whispery voice. "I've been trying to get you for the last half-hour."

"I've been on the phone with my parents. You know what that can be like?"

"Not really. I've never had that burden, since I never knew who my so-called parents were."

"But J.B.'s not your name?," I argued.

"It's convenient. As far back as I can remember it's been J.B., and it always will be. Can you handle that?"

This intimacy was so unexpected that I didn't know how to respond. "Are you calling from Pigtown?"

"I'm heading up your way after sundown. First things first. Congrats, your work on Randy paid off."

"In what way?"

"I've set up a meeting in Daddy's office tonight at 10. There's something I want to show both of you."

"Randy made contact with Broadway? Is that what you're saying?"

"Just be there. 10 pm sharp."

"I'll be there," I answered.

"See you," and he hung up.

For J.B., one thing was certain—J.B. was Daddy's own. I suppose, for him, that was sufficient personal contact.

I hit the pigeon shit at five of ten. Daddy and J.B. were in Daddy's office, ready to go. A portable TV and DVD player were set up.

"Before we get to the visuals," J.B. announced, "I'd like you to hear this Q-and-A I had with Randy after viewing what you'll be seeing. There's no sound on the video, and it will explain what you're about to watch."

There was a contained command and a sense of winning a prize in J.B.'s attitude I'd never seen before. New sides of J.B. were emerging from his assignment in Pigtown. It was pretty clear he had taken over my assignment there. For one, he radiated a sense of enjoyment—something one would never suspect him capable of. Daddy sat motionless in his chair. J.B. produced a small digital recorder from his jacket pocket. With a slight flourish, he placed it on Daddy's desk and pressed the play button. His was the first voice to be heard.

J.B.: "Randy, tell me how you managed to make contact with Broadway again."

Randy: "It happened so sudden-like. I almost didn't believe it." (He was still loud, but in better control than the last conversation I had with him.)

J.B.: "How did that happen?"

Randy: "He summoned me to his office for the day—a sauna or bath place. He changes offices two times a week. I knew he wanted something. He'd had an idea for a big party to honor his high-toned DC connections, but there was no one better than me to make it happen. I'd had such a good track record with him that he took to my ideas for the party and put me in charge of getting it all set up."

J.B.: "What sort of party are you talking about?"

Randy: "You remember my telling the detective at the federal building about my association with the stash houses before Big B put me onto the fetish action in town?"

J.B.: "You're referring to the 10-kilo drop-off ?"

Randy: "That's right. That was meant as a kind of promotion for me to get out to the main street. I'd had my fill of all the supervising the drop—offs. Once I got that going, I had time on my hands."

J.B.: "Let's get back to the party you mentioned."

Randy: "Mind you, J.B., I'd mentioned this idea to him before."

J.B: "What idea?"

Randy: "The DC upper—crust lappers ball."

J.B.: "When was that?"

Randy: "Round about two years ago. But the Bigness got cold feet thinking it might be putting him in a bad light, so he laid low on it. Meanwhile, he was pulling down low change on the operation as it was."

J.B.: "Tell me more about that."

Randy: "These local girls were working their tits off in those stash houses. Naked as the day they were born, banging away with hammers, picks and cheese graters to break those bricks down. And having to move the whole operation to other houses every time someone thought the law was watching."

J.B.: "Why naked?"

Randy: "To stop them from stealing the stuff for themselves."

J.B.: "They wouldn't have gotten away with it."

Randy: "So, what happens when the shit floats up in the air as they break bricks up all day?"

J.B.: "It lands on their bodies."

Randy: "You got it, I don't need to elaborate no further on the profit possibilities with pretty women coated in raw coke. Profits were good, but they were messing up by having these low level lappers at the door."

J.B.: "And so you raised the possibilities?"

Randy: "The grand gala for these lapping freaks came from me. The fetish was a big hit from Baltimore to DC, and with an invite only list, a buffet of girls, black, white, Spanish, from 16 years old to 30 in all their glory, it was easy to provide after a shipment got street ready."

Randy: "When the boss heard my idea, He couldn't resist it! He loved it—everything about it. He called it 'history repeating itself', like the Romans who combined sex with social activities. And if it was recorded in history books, why not add another chapter?"

J.B.: "How was it possible to get this video made? Was Broadway in on it?"

Randy: "In truth, it was his idea—to get a record of the reopening of his favorite project. As a souvenir, he could go back to it time and again . . . and get off on it each time."

J.B.: "And there were no complaints?"

Randy: "Not so far. I think the guests wearing the masks helped. That was B's idea."

J.B. "So you think some of those who might have complained came anyway?"

Randy: "They were more than curious, if you catch my meaning. And besides, what was there to lose? They got a free show, entirely paid for by Mr. B himself—this time—except the tips for the girls performing their human lollypop routines." (J.B. and Daddy looked at one another with deep satisfaction.)

J.B.: "You said there were invitations?"

Randy: "I collected them myself at the door. But the invitations had no names on them—that was only for the envelopes they were sent in."

J.B.: "Do you think they had any idea this event was being filmed?"

Randy: "No, not as far as I know. Only Broadway knew. He asked for it—asked me to find suitable personnel who could do it . . . and keep their mouths shut. They were paid big time."

J.B.: "Still, he was taking a chance . . ."

Randy: "Sure. He made one no-no. No copies were to be made. And he demanded the one, only, original print."

J.B.: "Every emperor has his tragic flaw. Answer me this last question, why didn't you answer Detective Larkin's question about all this when he asked?"

Randy: "I was hungry, that's why, and when I get hungry, that takes priority over everything else. Besides, this big party hadn't happened yet."

JB: "Yeah, you even preferred not to answer the lawyer's questions about it. After all, she got your sandwich."

Randy: "I was eating—and besides . . ."

JB: "Besides what?"

Randy: "Come on, you don't talk about that kind of kinky shit with no uptown lawyer woman. I may be from Pigtown, but I got manners. What do you take me for?"

JB: "But you were there to purposely answer . . ."

Randy: (voice rising) "You put shackles on my feet and threw me behind bars! At least allow me a bit of dignity."

JB: "I wonder where your dignity would have landed if this whole idea of yours folded—you were sticking your neck out."

Randy: "Isn't that what I'm supposed to do? Huh? Huh? I signed a paper with you boys, and I honor my commitments."

J.B.: "I repeat—you're still taking a big chance here."

Randy: "I've been there before. Besides, the Boss likes playing with White Boy. He gets his jollies that way, too. Sure, he'll find something to complain about after, and I'll be out shovelin' dirt somewhere until he needs me again. Well, this time he can go fuck himself. I hope when he goes down, he goes down real hard. And I want to be there when it happens."

This last pronouncement was yelled at top decibel, and the tape came to an end.

Daddy spoke up for the first time. "Good work. You can pass that along to Shooter. Frankly, the one I was most worried about was Randy, but it appears I might be wrong. Where was this video shot?"

J.B. replied, "Shooter—in a tux—mingled among the guests with a pinhole camera in his suit jacket. Randy arranged it all."

"Which hotel?"

"The Belvedere. One of the old-time places—with a huge ballroom and hanging chandeliers."

"I had no idea Broadway had any sense of history. But he obviously had a smattering of ignorance on the subject, wouldn't you say, Larkin?"

I replied, "I suppose so. The Belvedere is a relic of the thirties and forties—probably as close to an ancient setting in which to appease his vanity and peculiar tastes."

"Well, then, there you go."

Chapter Twenty-Six

There is a long lead into the video of walking on the street and through parking lots, people standing stationary intently watching the groups walk outside the hotel grounds. Lookouts, most likely—considering the clientele involved in the sex carnival inside. Then a murky shot of four homogenous chandeliers, looming over a candlelit corridor below. The chandeliers are dead, like the hotel itself—a relic of the past.

The corridor is crowded with guests, dressed in black suits and tuxedos, wearing small face masks. The image is ghostly as if we were seeing the same man in duplicate. Shooter is filming somewhere in this crowd, rigged up with the hidden camera, obviously high definition since the images were crystal clear. So far, the scenes look calm and atmospheric. Trays of wine and champagne pass overhead by barely discernable waiters. A great shot of a gaggle of men's hands reaching up for fresh champagne on a tray. As the camera moves at a steady unhurried pace, it pauses on one man talking to a small group.

J.B says, "That's Randy."

The transformation from slob to this is almost unbelievable. In prerequisite dress code, he laughs. There are five people clustered around him. The candlelight ambiance gives this shot a Fellini—like look (La Dolce Vita). On closer inspection, this group of five men are not men, but women dressed in black suits. Two, the younger of the five, even wear tophats no doubt to conceal their long hair. The other three are all middle-aged and wrinkled. The group keeps shifting around in place as they speak to Randy, checking the passersby as they converse. One of the younger "men" whispers into the ear of another, who turns her head to check someone out. What role does this group play in the upper DC crust? Cigarettes are being lit among the crowd, the size of which is somewhat difficult to figure out because it's so dim. The camera picks up a man throwing an arm around another's waist, mouths moving in rapid exchanges. Friends or social familiars no mask can hide? The two men wander away, and the camera takes a dive to the parquet floor littered by cigarette butts. Except for the apparel, no further formality is being observed, not to mention respect for the hotel Belvedere itself, known as the El Dorado of its day.

Suddenly, hands are seen applauding, and the camera shifts to find Broadway—the entrepreneur himself in a tuxedo so shiny that it appears

like a cutout from which his head protrudes. A jovial smile and popping eyes
catch him in pantomime addressing "his people". His expression indicates he is
dispensing homilies of some sort. He then gestures into the crowd before him
and beckons someone in its midst to come forward. The person indicated edges
his way toward Broadway. Shooter for some reason gets in a place behind him.
Broadway places his hands on the man's shoulders. We see the man's back, long
dark blond hair in a ponytail in close—up.

My heart starts to race. I turn away from the screen and look at Daddy and
J.B, then quickly look back at the screen.

The crowd is moving to a room off to the left, and Shooter follows. The
screen goes black.

J.B. speaks up again, "This is where Randy said Shooter took a designated
seat on the front right tier to shoot the rest."

In that respect, the whole place becomes an indoor Roman arena. Shooter
on his perch is safe from the lions.

The first victims into the arena are three ladies who on appearance look
phosphorescent—the effect of being immersed in white powder, likely cocaine
from the bagging houses, from head to toe. They all were stiletto high heels
and shiny tiaras on their heads and are completely bare—assed. They stand
together and strike a pose, gyrating slowly to reveal it all—then march to a
different area for others to view and repeat their pose.

J.B. stands center of the screen and, with one ass covering his chest, he says,
"The guests are seated in chairs under the boxed tiers."

Curious, I ask, "Are there only three lappettes for so many people?" That's
my term for those to be lapped.)

J.B put his finger on the play button ready to resume, Daddy seems amused
at all this display. "No" J.B answers, "There are nine all together. They appear
three at a time for the lucky numbers assigned." And the tableaux becomes live
again. It's Randy's turn again—he steps forward holding a woven basket in his
hand. Each lappette pick a number, and Randy calls them out. The camera
searches the area for the lucky ones. Then a quick turn to a full picture with
some new people standing by their goddesses. The camera focuses on a man

who takes off his jacket, removes his tie and opens the top button of his shirt. The goddess's shoes are off standing together. They appear to be portable banks for their earnings. There are already stacks of bills in one shoe. The man is lapping the girls left leg in short regular strokes; his manner is very businesslike, almost as if he was taking his daily supplements. The goddess does not move. He has lapped to her knee. The skin under the powder is black—and she looks as if she was wearing a black stocking. The man pauses, picks up his jacket and removes a flask from his inside pocket. He drinks a mouthful and washes down whatever residue of the drug was still in his mouth.

The camera moves back to the center of the room revealing a lesbian enclave. Grandma is sitting in a chair at her goddess breast level—the two older women's jackets have traces of the powder spotting them. They are lapping the right and left arms. Grandma picks up her bag, and removes several crisp bills from a side pocket and places them in one of the shoes, both of which are overflowing with cash. She then puts her mouth over the goddesses left nipple and begins sucking it like a child. The goddess right arm, now completely lapped, pats the old woman's head. Her arm is a slightly off—shade white. Asien maybe? The full image of the goddess and the three women lapping at her body delicately is positively surreal fetish porn.

The camera glides over to the left side of the room to find two men of medium height and curly heads (Could be brothers? if so, the old adage comes to mind, "The family that laps together, stays together.") Others seem to have some routine to their work, intent on creating connecting designs with their tongues. This goddess is white on white and her two shoes are filled with bills—in fact, she is already smiling. Her arms, now finished off, are at her sides. The two men are working on her navel and at one point their tongues touch each other and remain in that position for a run down her body. (What am I looking at?)

Suddenly the screen goes completely blank. J.B. gets up and stops the machine, saying, "Shooter, in a hurry to get there, grabbed an uncharged battery. He was afraid to go to the men's room to call someone to get him a new battery or leave and go back inside. Broadway had this place being watched from every angle, and Randy was nowhere to be found."

A long silence fell between us—my thoughts were stumbling over themselves. My initial prurient interest had quickly dispatched itself. All I was left with was my rage at what I'd witnessed. This event was not a sometime thing. What other fun and games were on Broadway's prospectus for his people? Every person there to participate or watch was an experienced thrill seeker—a member of the DC cash—infused fetish scene courted by Broadway for his nefarious purposes. These people had a finger in the political pie which was DC's elite. The very idea left me in a state of despair for the course of power affecting our lives, now and in the future.

My second concern was for the man with the pigtail. "J.B." I asked, "Do you know if the guy with the pony tail showed up again?" Daddy cracked his knuckles for the first time, "Why do you ask son? To answer the question not being asked. Yes, that was Frank you saw."

I'd given myself away by my initial response to his appearance on screen . . . and by not asking the real question concerning his identity. I had been admonished now, as on several occasions. I found rebukes of this order a kind of overkill of protocol, particularly given my coverage of Pigtown.

Daddy rose from his chair and moved slowly to the now-empty screen. He remained there with his back to us. When he turned round, he had removed his shades and started to wipe them with a handkerchief from his pocket. He didn't look at us as he spoke. He just kept rubbing his lenses. "Now, the next step is to find out if another of these parties is to take place soon . . ."

"I don't think we can risk getting another video," J.B. spoke up.

"Another video is not necessary—it will only be another version of the one we just saw." He paused, rubbed on silently, and then put his shades back on before facing us. "We have to find ways of identifying some of the people who attended."

Neither J.B. nor I said anything.

"Particularly those with DC license plates. Get them out from under those masks."

"What have you in mind?," J.B. asked, with a tinge of alarm in his voice.

"We've got to manage to get pictures—stills, shot from a distance, close-ups—we can study. We can replay this video and watch more closely.

Besides Shooter, are any of the other boys on the team skilled enough with a camera?"

"I can check," J.B. volunteered.

"And I want you to talk to Randy. See what he can do about finding the names and addresses on the envelopes containing invitations. Tell him that Daddy would be more than pleased if he could manage to do so. Tell him I would show my special appreciation in that eventuality."

("How?" I thought. "With a full pardon?")

"What if this fetish party we saw was a one-time thing?," I spoke up.

"From J.B.'s Q-and-A, I'd hold an opposite opinion. And Broadway has had a singular success with his night at the Belvedere. As Pigtown's Roman King, he's bound to indulge his appetite as often as the yen for it tickles his fancy."

"What about Frank?" J.B. inquired quietly.

"I've not decided yet about him getting involved."

"He's obviously close to the boss. Why not . . . ?"

"Too close. That's the problem."

What could Daddy be inferring with that statement? "'Too close?' That was the idea, wasn't it?," I asked.

"Nonetheless, I think Randy's our man," Daddy said dismissively. "He, too, is also close to Broadway at the moment and also master of the revels. While Broadway depends on Randy's know-how, Randy can take advantage and find ways of uncovering the information we need."

"How?" J.B. and I said it together.

"By developing the art of lapping to an even more specialized level. If I were Broadway," Daddy mused, with a half-smile, "I'd want to be part of some one-time thrill—a thrill he alone could provide his clientele. Randy could encourage Broadway in that direction, and Broadway then would leave it up to Randy to find out the special trick that would get Mr. and Mrs. DC really off. By doing that, he'd have to rely on Randy's scouting out what that special thing could be. And by doing that, Broadway would have to supply Randy with certain necessary data. In the land of perversity, there is no bottom that cannot be catered to by those who seek it. And those who cater to it."

J.B. looked at me, then back to Daddy. "It's worth a try."

Daddy turned to me. "John, how does this strategy strike you?"

"I can't help thinking that, felon or not, we promised Randy a chance to get out from under and make a life for himself. Your idea puts him at maximum risk."

"But he is already at maximum risk as it is," Daddy continued jovially. "Might as well get the most we can out of the situation." He studied me for a moment. "I'm surprised at you, son. I would have thought you'd understood that principle by now."

THE
CLOTHES

Chapter Twenty-Seven

The late August heat continued on relentlessly, as did the silence that prevailed at S.I.S. No news of any kind, other than the initial report J.B. sent to Daddy, "Randy promises to try." I was at the office the morning that it arrived. I'd overstepped the bounds of my position at S.I.S by intercepting the report before Daddy had reached the office. My reaction to his suggestion about Randy being put into a dangerous corner had suddenly put me on the outs again—a position that not only rankled, but felt like out-and-out abuse. Daddy was barely civil. I wanted to call J.B. himself, who was now fully invested in my former position as leader of the team. I dialed, then hung up, knowing that any inquiries I'd make would be reported to Daddy. And I existed in some no man's land in the chain of command over activities in Operation White Shadow. All this was, of course, only partly about Randy—it was Frank I wanted to hear about.

Then, one night, there came a pure Iraqi dream. I saw Frank running—running away from someone or something chasing him over the sand. Frank's mouth was open in a nightmare shriek—but, there was no sound, and I heard instead a voice calling out, "John!" I sat up immediately in my bed. The voice, a real voice, seemed to have sounded literally by my bedside, an echo of it still vibrating in the silent room. I continued listening, both hoping and yet fearing I'd hear that "John!" again. I couldn't identify whose voice it was, but it was a man's voice.

Marie was asleep next to me. I carefully rose out of bed, went into the bathroom, dressed hastily and left the apartment.

I got into my car and drove. I felt numb. I felt I also didn't know what I was doing, where I was going. Everything around me and outside in the darkness threatened. Frank's running image returned, and I stopped driving. I looked around me—nothing seemed familiar. Was I really here . . . wherever that was? Or was I dreaming still? I felt an unexpected chill in the sultry air and headed back to my car. I sat behind the wheel, waiting for light to break. It was 2:28 am by my watch. I rested my head against the wheel and promptly fell into a tense sleep.

Later that night, as I slept, Frank was killed. I was to discover he lay dead hardly twenty minutes away. In a wild attempt to reach Frank, I had driven close to the edge of Pigtown.

My search had come full circle, to a dead stop. All the evidence was in—Frank at the hospital, my eulogy, the burial, my anguished return to S.I.S after the cemetery, Frank's last will and testament—and I now none the wiser as to who had killed my bro. It had been a futile exercise, like rearranging the deckchairs on the Titanic. The ship foundered and disappeared forever.

I thought fleetingly of the team. Was it still in operation? Had Randy succeeded in convincing Broadway to upscale the freak show? Anyway, it was all over. I was out of the loop and didn't care to follow up on any of it. I thought of my Marie, with full intention of devoting my time to her. After all, as per my agreement with Daddy, I was on "stress leave". And while rejecting it on principle, I intended to take advantage of it and stay away from S.I.S and everything about it that encroached on my life and well-being. Weeks of deadly silence and numbness followed. Frank had been buried at the end of August—here we were now in only October. Frank's death was now history—but for me, it was still appallingly alive.

Chapter Twenty-Eight

Marie was already dressed and on her way to the hospital. But she was now standing at the side of my bed, shaking me gently awake. As always, I checked my wristwatch. It was 6:37 in the morning, and Marie was looking down at me with a worried expression on her face. "John, I think it's him on the phone."

"Who?"

Sigh. "Daddy. He insists on talking to you."

"On what phone?" And I looked at the bedside one. It was still on its cradle.

"Your cell. I heard it ringing in your jacket in the living room.

I immediately hopped out of bed, threw on my robe and pushed myself awake. I sat on the couch with the cell. "Hello," I said, feigning alertness. Marie placed a cup of her coffee on the table beside me.

"Son, as you know, I'm a very patient man and have sympathized with your need to push recent events to the side."

"I appreciate your understanding, sir."

"But we had a very clear understanding. You even asked for a letter, which I gave you. And yet you've done nothing about it?"

"I'm sorry. I've just gotten up and don't catch your drift, sir."

"You've made no effort to follow through, damn it."

I waited him out.

"So, for the last time, son, do you or do you not wish to claim Officer Dixon's clothes and personal effects?"

"Sir, as I said, I fully intend to . . ."

"Well, I'm glad to hear that, because—believe it or not—I didn't intend to jump your prerogative in the matter. But time's up, John. As of this morning, the Pigtown apartment under Dixon's name is no longer under his name. I've been informed by the landlord it's been returned to its former status."

I tried in the interim to swallow some coffee to bring me to full consciousness. "I'm sorry. I can't quite follow you, sir."

"You're always full of apologies, son, but I'm willing to follow you on the road of grief only so far."

"I'll be there to pick up his things. If you will tell me where I need to go . . ."

"Right outside your front door to the street."

"What? Sir, come again?"

"J.B. was good enough to take them to you himself. You can thank him personally for his indulgence."

I was dumbfounded by this bizarre largesse. But then, Daddy wasn't Daddy for nothing.

"Well, get to it! J.B.'s waiting."

"Thank you, sir. I do thank you."

"For what?," came the sharp retort.

"For your consideration . . . in not dumping his personal stuff."

"I had no intention of dumping anything."

"Or whatever else you had in mind other than consigning them to me. I still don't believe he's gone. Sorry, sir." An unintended slip I couldn't prevent. (The prick!)

"Gone is gone, John." Daddy's voice evened out. "I made this decision out of no sentimentality on my part, but out of respect for your value and achievements."

"Thank you, sir."

"I have only one other cavil with you. Need I name it?"

"No, sir. I will attend to it, too."

"Good." And he hung up, as I did. The cavil? The burn box.

My only thought was that this was Daddy's ongoing vigilante move to eradicate all evidence of Frank's connection to S.I.S. What really happened to provoke his frantic zeal?

It took J.B. and myself twenty minutes to unload the car of Frank's clothes and to dump them all on the living room floor. Marie had already left for work. J.B. and I had not exchanged a word during this move, except for his parting shot. "Have you checked the bottoms of your shoes lately? Might need attending?" And he slouched into his car. J.B. had returned to his former self. He leaned out of the car window for a postscript.

"Hey, John!" I paused with my arms full of the last bit of Frank's clothing. "Here's a little P.S. from Daddy. Dixon's funds from the credit union have now been transferred to your account. Have fun!"

This "psychological move" on Daddy's part served to convince me that some Pigtown fungus had sprouted at S.I.S and that I was being both provoked and tantalized toward some unchartered waters.

I did what I could putting Frank's clothes away. Daddy had mentioned memorabilia, but there was no evidence of such. I recalled a few framed citations, but there were none in this collection of his things. Most of his clothes I hung in a closet in the den. A few suits went into our bedroom closet. There was now practically no room for any new acquisitions of our own. I did all this mechanically, not wanting to search pockets for forgotten items. There was a naphthalene smell to the clothes, as if they had been dry-cleaned before being shipped over. I noticed three silk suits—an innovation for Frank. I remembered

Broadway emerging out of the cocoon of his chariot in Pigtown, in a blast of silk.

I got myself in order and went down to Jimmy's for breakfast, then sat in the park watching the early-autumn leaves. I didn't go near S.I.S. Didn't call in either. Spent my afternoon watching another bad movie—where I was overwhelmed by the thought that Operation White Shadow had now totally impinged not only on my life, but Marie's. I wanted to rush home and work out another solution about storing Frank's clothes, but I felt paralyzed, unable to think straight. Anything I did now other than keeping his clothes where I had consigned them would feel like a rejection of Frank. This was what was left of my brother. I was helpless at the moment to sully that bond. The thought of storing them in some anonymous warehouse was unthinkable.

I feared Marie's reaction when she came home. She'd seen J.B.'s car out front. My fealty to the S.I.S code of silence had preempted our lives so completely that I found myself more and more censoring my thoughts and impulses; and the heated recollections in my journal—such as these—continued to add more coal than the grate can bear. I realized in an instant the reason I had delayed picking up Frank's effects was the added burden it would place on Marie. Much as she loved him as a friend and my bro, the living proof of his death would become stifling. The secrets of my life as a cop were pushing her up against a brick wall.

On arrival, her first question related to this morning's call and the monster car parked out front. When I explained, she immediately went to the den. I sat on the couch with a coffee mug in my hand and waited. When she came back, I was not prepared for what she brought in with her. She was holding a lady's white dress suspended between her fingers.

She lifted it and said, "The world is truly an amazing place. You learn a little something new every day. Can you picture Frank in this?"

I considered that possibility in a fit of lunacy.

"Marie, is this a joke? Where did you find that? Or is it yours or what?"

She placed the dress against her own body. It was plainly an impossible supposition on my part.

"It was tangled up under a pair of trousers and jacket." And she finally burst into irrepressible laughter.

"Yes, I think I saw that dress once." And I was relieved of my mad vision. "It belongs to Marjorie Wyatt."

"The tattooed lady?"

"The same. She must have left it in his closet and forgotten it was there."

"And now she's here! And he's all here, too!"

"There's more in our room," I added sheepishly. She just glowered at me. "It was all left to me . . . in his will."

"Secrets unfolding, right?" Marie said. "And what else are you holding back?"

I sighed and, unable to repress this corner of mystery, told Marie all there was to know about the burn box. Protocol no longer seemed to matter at this point.

"It was to be the same way round should I . . . instead of Frank," I said, almost pleading. "I'll move it somewhere else. I thought you'd, well, understand."

"When have I ever not understood? It comes with the territory. And what do you intend to do with all this?"

"I don't know."

"What were you intending to do with them originally?"

I opened my hands in an empty gesture.

"Well, Johnny, let me know when you do. Right now, I'm hungry."

"So am I," I echoed.

"Let's not go out to dinner—I'm tired. There are some ribs in the freezer."

And suddenly we were all over each other, love hunger preempting stomach hunger.

Things happen in bunches, so it seems. Throw out a small hint to the universe, and it takes you up on it. Five days after the incident with the white dress, the owner herself made a call. And there was Marie by my bedside again—at a more reasonable hour—holding my cell phone out to me.

"Tell her I've had it dry-cleaned." And she dropped the cell into my lap and went back to her kitchen.

Indeed, it was Marjorie Wyatt herself, asking if we could meet somewhere tomorrow for a drink, lunch or both. She sounded formal, yet upbeat. "I'm only here through tomorrow. I hoped I could see you."

For some reason, I agreed. "Tomorrow then," I responded. She suggested the bar at the Marriott Inner Harbor, a posh place in the center of town. I would return the dress, and perhaps she had some news about Frank I didn't know. I hung up, wondering whether the white dress did belong to her.

Chapter Twenty-Nine

When I came out for my first coffee next morning, Marie was tidying up before she left for work. She had already brought out the white dress in a dry-cleaned, cellophane wrapper, "One Day Service." I explained today's lunch date. I was repeating myself—Marie said nothing. There had been a week's lull between our lovemaking, and I knew that the bliss, needing to be repeated, couldn't be expected so soon. The stress put on our lives had made its own secret inroads. A sort of listlessness hung between us. We were being caught up in the messy business of trying to maintain connection when our instincts pleaded for us to flee—leave—go. We were living and loving in an S.I.S of our own.

I arrived at the hotel ten minutes early, instructing the maitre d' I was expecting a lady, to discover the lady was already there expecting me. We hadn't talked to one another in nearly a year, but she smiled in recognition as I approached her table. It was now middle October, and the trees lining the Inner Harbor where in fall blaze. Marjorie was out of her slumming attire and sat there in a rather smart-looking blue, two-piece outfit which was seasonally appropriate. There was no possibility of her revealing her no-no's, a factor I had dreaded encountering again. She beckoned me to sit opposite her at the table. I had been here often—it was one of Frank's hotels. The first thing I noticed was how clean-faced and relaxed Marjorie seemed. She had dropped her tough-guy stance, and her aristocratic features were an almost startling surprise.

"You're looking well, John. I may call you 'John'?" she asked, putting down her glass of white wine, to shake my hand.

"If that's the case, you're looking even better," I replied, sitting opposite her. A tiny nod passed for a thank you. The waiter had been signaled by Marjorie, and he was at my side. I didn't recognize him. He was daytime staff.

"Please, this is on me," Marjorie added quickly. "You're my guest—you're welcome to stay for lunch if it suits you." Marjorie Wyatt was living up to her name and class, with a sobriety and delicacy she had long kept under wraps. As I ordered a Jim Beam Black and Diet Coke, Marjorie studied me with an inquiring look. We lifted glasses and drank a nameless toast.

"Have you married your lady yet? She sounds charming. In all that's happened this year, I'm not sure whether you have or not."

"Not yet," I responded.

"Frank said he thought you'd never marry . . . although you had met the lady of your life."

"Marjorie, please—why did you ask me here?"

"I see you're not inclined to social amenities," and she picked up her glass.

"I'm as good at it as any," and sipped my drink against a temptation to empty the glass.

"Or maybe it's just me. We never did hit it off, did we?"

"No, I'm afraid not," I conceded.

"Well, thank you for being honest."

"Then permit me to ask again . . ."

"To give you something," she said pleasantly, even wistfully.

"Oh? What?"

"I was with Frank the day before he was killed. He wanted to be sure, if anything happened to him, I'd get to you." Suddenly, she drank down the rest of her white wine and closed her eyes. When she looked at me, her lips were drawn, and she shrugged her shoulders. For a moment, she was the old she.

"That's more like it—is that what you're thinking?" And her nails elicited a ping from her empty glass. "Down—the—hatch me, that is. Well, let me tell you that will never happen again. It won't. You're part of my saying goodbye to my . . . lifestyle of late, shall we say."

"What's the catch, Marjorie?" I ventured.

"Catch? There is no catch! I just wanted to say goodbye to Baltimore—and to old acquaintances—before I make a clean break with it. You were the last one on my list."

"Thank you."

"Only because you were the closest of all to Frank—and would help me feel he was still with us. You see, under all my pretenses, I'm rather an old-fashioned girl . . . of the old school? And also because—I've told no one else but my immediate family—I'm pregnant."

I looked at her levelly and thought, "Here it comes—the plea for money." And she savaged that thought with her next remark.

"I'm not wanting anything from you, John."

"Pregnant?" I repeated.

"Yes, and it's Frank's."

I didn't know what to say that wouldn't sound patronizing or downright offensive. So I said nothing.

"I was with Frank all during the case you guys were working. I knew you were involved but didn't have any contact with Frank. He wanted to find a way to make contact with you, but he was afraid Mr. Broadway had eyes everywhere."

"Who killed him?" I asked—my obsession speaking.

"I . . . I'm not sure. Maybe in the book, but whoever it was . . ."

"What book?," I almost demanded.

"Frank kept a private diary besides sending his reports to S.I.S. He told me it contains information he never included in his reports. I have not read it, I swear—it was meant for you. Frank wanted you to have it. He made me promise I'd get it to you if . . ." And she bit her lips to hold back tears. "I think I'd better order lunch," and she beckoned to the waiter.

"Maybe another glass of wine would help," I said. Bastard me.

"No—no more wine. One is enough. I'm turning a new page, speaking of books."

And she ordered lunch.

"Won't you join me?," she asked gently as the waiter hovered.

"Yes, another one of these. No, make it a Jim Beam black . . . straight."

Marjorie smiled sympathetically as the waiter glided away.

"We were intending to leave Pigtown and reconstitute somewhere else. I suggested my hometown in Maine. Do you know Maine?"

"My family has a place in Kennebunkport. Have had it since I was a boy," I said. But I was thinking of the book.

"How serendipitous."

"Go on about Frank."

"He was in very bad shape. I did what I could, but Frank needed to make a real break with his assignment. One day, he suddenly packed his clothes and disappeared on me for over three weeks."

"Where did he go?"

"I never found out, then one day he called me and asked me to meet him at his former apartment in town."

"But he'd already left it," I said.

"He told me he still had the key to his old place—had inquired about going back to it—and to meet him there. He sounded rather odd . . . strange."

"Strange? How?"

"It didn't sound like him, but he wouldn't take 'no' for an answer. He said we'd make more definite plans once we met. I know it all sounds crazy, but given what he went through . . ." She closed her eyes against it. She resisted going on about Frank and kept shaking her head, as if to deny the import of her thoughts.

Rather than push her further, I decided to wait until she was ready to go on.

"Are you going back to Maine now?" I asked.

"Yes," and she brightened. "I come from well-to-do people, John. Despite my trip of the light fantastic, my family has been my constant support throughout—financially and otherwise. They've asked me to come home and have my baby."

"Were you and Frank formally . . . ?"

"No, we never married. I knew the hint of marriage would have scared Frank off. Did you know anything about his childhood? His family? He never spoke of them. He said once he didn't want to remember 'all that sordid stuff', as he put it."

"I know even less than you on that score. I could only intuit it was less than 'pleasant', to use a euphemism."

"You know, John, I'll confess something to you. All during these last few years, I was secretly jealous of you."

"Jealous? Why jealous? Because of Marie?"

"No, because of you. You and Frank shared a bond—a brotherly love—that touched me deeply and, yes, made me angry that I could not share it." Marjorie and Marie both now had expressed this same sentiment to me. "But as far as brotherly love is concerned, I, too, have an older brother, and he was the one who persuaded me to come back."

"What? To share his brotherly love with you?" I said it—not intending to be negative—but not knowing what else to say to the woman at this point.

"My older brother is starting a new practice . . . in dentistry. He wants me to be one of his assistants."

"Dentistry? What do you know about dentistry?"

"I know the power of an anesthetic. No, I meant it practically." She smiled.

"You see, I've had training in it—but, after college, turned the possibility of becoming a professional down. You can now definitely imagine me in my white smock and white hose and sensible shoes—the whole image covering up all the physical prizes embedded in my skin." She touched her covered shoulder delicately.

"I intend to actually get rid of them . . . over time. Certainly after my child is born I will see to it. My brother knows a doctor who can accomplish this miracle. It will be really like shedding my old skin!" She obviously knew what I felt—and what I'd been feeling—since I first met her.

"When are you leaving?"

"Tomorrow. I'll be in Maine by the next morning."

"Marjorie, I want you to know that, in a pact made a long time ago between Frank and myself, he left whatever was in his bank account to me should there be a . . ."

"John, how generous of you, but as I told you . . ."

"Perhaps we can think of a way to put it to use. A college fund. A bequest from his father to . . ."

"Yes, you're right. It will be a boy. I know that much at least. I'm over three months along." She gestured with her hand, then looked in her carryall. Took a small pad and pen, wrote something on it, and placed it in front of me. It was an address—hers, in Maine.

Lunch arrived and was served in silence. Marjorie picked up her fork, but it lay there between her fingers. She seemed intent on something other than food.

"He told me he might not survive this case and that it was not safe for me to be seen with him . . . anywhere. I asked why. He said it was dangerous for me—in Pigtown or outside. That's why. I never showed up for the eulogy or the burial. I wished I had now."

"Did you catch up with him? At his apartment?"

"I drove to it, yes. He called—it was about two or three in the morning—and said I was to meet him at our 'appointed place'. He put it that way, as if he feared being overheard by someone other than myself. When I got there, his car was parked out front. I rang his doorbell. There was no answer, so I opened the door and went in. I smelled fresh paint, but Frank was not there. I then went out back to his car. The car keys were still in the ignition. There was something so . . . so menacing about it all. I'm afraid I panicked—I did—and I left. I waited for him to call again, but he never did. Next day, I read he had been . . ."

Her fork was still where it was, poised and now trembling. She let go of the fork and pressed her fingers against the table to steady them.

I placed my hand over her tense fingers.

"Your lunch is getting cold."

Her fingers went back into action with a delicate grace, although her fork merely prodded her food. I picked up my Jim Beam.

"Happy tidings from now on, Marjorie. I mean it." And drank my lunch.

"Oh," she said, "how forgetful of me." Turning round, she rummaged inside her bag and came up with a stiff-backed book, presumably Frank's diary.

"And this goes with it," she said, handing over the book and a small envelope. I placed the book next to me, pocketed her address and picked up the envelope. The moment I touched it, I knew what it contained, even before opening it. I simply stared at Marjorie. She looked up and read what was in my face.

"John, I understand. I'm used to eating alone. Mission accomplished—no need to stay. Just one more thing—do let us keep in touch. Please," she said with great intensity. "You're the only living person I know who knew him."

I rose and nodded slowly.

"Thanks for lunch," and I shook my head. I was feeling washed out and, in a fit of bad manners, left to go.

The moment I sat in the car, I opened the envelope. I shook its contents into my hand. It was the lost, white rosary that had mysteriously disappeared from my old Toyota. I placed Frank's diary on the seat next to me and saw Marjorie's dry-cleaned dress awaiting its delivery. I almost brought it back to her, but decided it was too late—and certainly too intimate a gesture—and, should it not be hers, an embarrassment. I decided to send it to her via the address she'd just given me. I picked up the diary from my lap, put it in my lap and took off.

Chapter Thirty

That night, I told Marie everything about the case. It was my first full act of disobedience against the code. Marie's face never left mine, and she heard me to the end. I then pulled the rosary out of my pocket and dangled it.

"It was Frank who took it out of my car. I think, in returning it through Marjorie, he was telling me it was he who saved my life that day."

"Are you sure?" Marie said quietly.

"No, but maybe after I read his diary, I'll find out."

"So then it's your turn again, Johnny, I guess. At least in the deadly games you guys play."

"Yes. The only trouble is that his life is already gone. There's nobody or anything left to be salvaged. I can't save him. I can't save any of the others." (Thinking of Randy at that moment.)

"Yes, there is someone."

"Who?"

"Me, Johnny."

"You? I never thought that way about you—not in that way."

"Well, start thinking about it." And she rose and said, "I'm not talking relationship only. It's this city—this awful, corrosive city—that has completely undermined all my good intentions for it. It's left a trace of itself in me I just can't erase. And if it's happening here, it must be in other places—places becoming another Baltimore. What's to stop it happening? And what do I do then . . . when it does? What does anyone do?"

I'd never seen Marie so withdrawn from herself. For the first time, I feared for her safety and wellbeing. "I'm too tired to go out," she said. "I'm not hungry."

"Shall I . . . ?"

"No, you have other things to do." And she nodded towards Frank's diary on the table.

"I'm not hungry," I said lamely and sat down heavily on the couch with the diary in my hands. I heard the lock of the bedroom door click in. Marie had left me to my obsession and with her last question to me left unanswered. I went into the den—now practically Frank's room—and started reading.

At past 2 am, I went back to the living room and tried to get some sleep on the couch. Sleep? After what I'd just read? Impossible!

FRANK'S
DIARY

Chapter Thirty-One

. . . .

Frank's diary is medium-sized. Bound in black leather, it resembles some oversized prayer manual with a zipper. The end papers are coal black. The white pages are lined and bound within its covers.

First Page

> *Bro, this is for you. Half of what's in these pages has been in Daddy's hands as part of my daily reports to him. I wrote them—not seeing you and missing you and afraid I might never see you again.*

Second Page

A small photograph—scotch-taped to the page—cut from a larger photo. A woman's arm is visible in the right-hand corner. "Frank Keaton", his cover name, is under the photo. The ordinary cover name contrasts sharply with the new cover look. In his favor—as against mine—Frank possesses a head of hair that is his obedient servant, his dark-blond mane responding to his need for change with convincing results. The guiding idea behind the new identity was to associate the look with someone who drove a commercial truck for a living. The model: The elements suggesting some mullet-headed, redneck, country-music type. "Redneck" also implies "racist", and I'm sure that would not have sat well with the kingpin. Frank managed to turn these requirements into assets, while preserving a prototypical look. He resembled a rock star, photographed after a night of drinking, at a local diner eating breakfast. Pony-tailed, western-shirted, Frank had also grown a thin goatee mustache that was neatly trimmed—the whole actually graced with a ruffian-style hairdo crowning a clean, well-groomed face.

Page Three And On

I shift to my sober side to let you know how it's happening and how much I'm thinking of you along the way. This journal can never find its way to prosecutors, because it will taint Daddy's case so badly that all of our sacrifices will have been for nothing. John, if something happens to me, I hope you get your hands on this. Read it, then burn it. I'm depending on M. to help. Forgive her tattoos, as God forgives sins.

Week 1

Bro, I got the job because I could drive a commercial truck and that's the long and short of it. When I asked about you, Daddy gave me the no contact routine to prevent case contamination and anyone who could compromise my cover—you heard him, but I figured Daddy wouldn't have lectured us about Operation White Shadow if he didn't have something in mind for you. Latrell came along in the assignment—he was to introduce me to Broadway and start the operation rolling. I had a lot of work to do to set up a legit trucking company and build a real person around my undercover identity.

Broadway is not one of your typical drug dealers. He likes to have the finer things in life, but wants them in private. He always travels with a small entourage that is more like a security detail than anything. When Broadway goes out to eat, he goes to the same places and has a table in the back of the room or in a private VIP area of the establishment. This allows him not only to do business in private, but gives him a view of who is in the room with him—much like when cops in uniform sit down to eat a meal. You know how we always sit in the back of the restaurant, backs against the wall, looking at everyone in front of us, including the front door. Broadway set up a meeting with Latrell and me at an old Italian mob restaurant in Little Italy that was famous for a salad called "the Bookmaker".

Latrell and I walked into the restaurant a little after ten o'clock. We were fifteen minutes late, figuring that showing up on time looks too eager. I knew what Broadway looked like from photographs but had to act as if I wasn't sure which guy he was. As Latrell led me to the second floor, I could feel my heart beating in my chest. It was a familiar feeling of anticipation and nervousness, but nonetheless controllable. After reaching the second floor, Latrell led us to the back of the building, which I noticed was a completely separate part of the restaurant with a separate back staircase leading to the kitchen. There was one large black guy standing next to the staircase and three others sitting at a round table in the corner of the room. My eyes turned toward the table, where I immediately recognized Broadway, but gave him the same little attention as the other two sitting with him. Latrell walked around the table and singled Broadway out, giving him a combination handshake and hug. All the while, Broadway never spoke a word or moved out of his chair. After giving him the greeting, the same was done—with much less respect—to the other two men before introducing me. Latrell pointed to me and said, "This is the guy I was telling you about." As I moved around the table to shake Broadway's hand, I was quickly stopped by the security element and thoroughly checked. All the while, Broadway was watching me, as if he was studying my reaction to this treatment. I did what I knew best when I was in a pinch—made a joke. "Man, you're treating me like a Muslim at the airport." After being checked by the guards, both left the table and took positions outside the room.

We sat down, flanking Broadway, with the gaudiest Italian setting in front of us. The waiter came up the stairs from the kitchen and placed several bottles of red wine on the table. He handed us a menu, then quickly exited down the stairs. There were at least four bottles of what looked like *different vintage wines and a tray of large glasses to go with them. A waiter systematically opened all four bottles. I was wondering why Broadway had not said anything yet and decided to take the initiative. "Mr. Broadway, I appreciate your fine taste in wine. Those look expensive, but, if you don't mind, I'll just have a Bud." Broadway looked up at me with one eye, at first with a look of disappointment, but eased into a smile and said in a surprisingly soft voice, "I thought all white people drank wine. Guess that's not the case." I laughed, taking advantage of him breaking the ice. "Look, I'm just a poor boy from New York trying to make money. I'm no different than you. I appreciate your hospitality, though. Your cousin has been a good friend to me." Broadway looked over at his cousin Latrell staring at the menu. "Yeah, he likes to be a little businessman, don't you, boy? Look, I don't know you from Adam, but I trust those who work for me or else you wouldn't even be in this room. I needed to lay my eyes on you to make sure, though." I asked the question even though I knew the answer, "Make sure of what?" Broadway took a long sip of one of his wines. "You know what I have become in this business? I have become a master of human behavior. I have seen fear, happiness, truth and lies and smelled the last fucking breath before the lights go out for good. I have a good instinct about people and can smell if they intend to bring harm to my way of life." I spoke right up, "Look, Mr. Broadway, I can tell you that I bring nothing but solutions to some of your transportation problems. I'm a businessman and a professional. There is no doubt that, in this business, you can't be too cautious; but, in this case, I don't come to you without a proven track record. Your cousin can vouch for that. What I can offer is guaranteed transport. We take the risks; you pay for that risk and, in turn, take no responsibility for any loss." Broadway looked at me as if I hit the magic button. "What do you mean by 'no responsibility for any loss'?" I used this to sink the hammer, "What I mean is, if a load is lost due to circumstances I can't control, we guarantee its value will be returned to you. For this guarantee, the price* will be higher per shipment, the loads bigger and profits for you through the roof. I wouldn't guarantee this service if I wasn't sure I could deliver. I have routes all over." Broadway put his hand up and stopped me mid-sentence. "Don't tell me anymore, Frankie. That way, if you fuck up a load, it's on you, bro, and I have no knowledge of how it was done." I looked at Broadway with a smile and an understanding that I most likely had the job. "Fair enough. I guess this calls for a celebration then." Broadway sat up in his chair and yelled down the staircase, "Yo, Vinnie, bring us three Buds!" Meanwhile, Broadway drank from the other three wine bottles. It looked like a ritual of some kind. First, he smelled each red, like a connoisseur, then down the hatch, his lidded eyes savoring the impact.

The rest of the night was no talk of business, just a lot of background questions about my life. Broadway was very inquisitive about my being a soldier and fighting in Iraq. Broadway seemed to actually like me by the night's end—he really paid little attention to Latrell. It seemed that all the background information—some truth, some lies—flowed in an even story that was seamless. The only thing out of place was the fact that Latrell sat there most of the time just listening. I even excused myself from the table to take a leak so Latrell would be forced to talk to Broadway. Before leaving the restaurant, Broadway stood up and shook my hand. He also told me to stop calling him "Mister". He wanted to be called by his much-deserved street name, "Boss Man".

After leaving the restaurant, I jumped on Latrell, pushing him up against a wall. "What the fuck is wrong with you? Are you trying to fuck this whole thing up? Goddammit, you looked like you were fucking wired or something." Latrell bowed his head down and let out a sob, "Frank, I'm sorry, this shit's got me scared. Yo, this dude is no joke. When he finds out that I set him up with you, I'm dead. I just signed my death warrant, and I didn't even say a fucking word." I let go of his shirt. "Relax, we'll take care of you now. You *know that there is no turning back. Even if you bail now, when we take him down, he'll still figure out you set him up with me, but you won't have our protection. Whether you like it or not, we need each other, and now is not the time to get cold feet. Brother, we are in with this cat! He loves me!"* Latrell, with a sobbing smile and short laugh, agreed, *"Yeah, you right, Frankie. He bit hard on you. That shit you made up about Iraq was insane. He loves that military shit."* I looked straight into his eyes and said, *"I didn't make those stories up . . . Let's get out of here—I need a drink."*

Week 4

John, I fell into the pigpen slops. And if Hell has stations, what came next was only the first stop.
Broadway would summon me—or "Frankie", as I was already donned—several times a week. I believe that Broadway actually enjoyed my company, but would also revisit things we already discussed, almost as if he was testing me to see if the story changed. I was solid in every lie that I told Broadway—every detail of that lie had some truth to it or paperwork to back it up. Besides wines, Broadway also had a fetish for strippers. He was different than most of the black kingpin crowd that would only frequent black establishments on the block—Broadway loved Russian women. At least twice a week, Broadway would get a private VIP suite at the Russian Tea Room, ironically on Broadway Street. This place is like the Beluga of strip clubs. The women are all Russian and as hot as you can get. Broadway would spend upwards of ten grand a night in the VIP room with all the trimmings. Broadway had me meet him in the VIP suite without Latrell being invited. When I walked into the dimly-lit room—after being searched by Broadway's dogs outside—Broadway was sitting on a large, red, satin couch with three of the most beautiful women draped over him, wearing nothing but their panties. One was rubbing his arms, another was curled up in his lap, and the other was feeding him sips of aged cognac. "Hey,

Boss Man, got some room in there for me?" Broadway, not
moving a muscle, "Frankie, pick one—anyone—of these
ladies. Except for the one on my lap—she's keeping me
warm." I looked at the remaining two. Both were equally
gorgeous, and I eventually picked one.

The girl got up and took me by the hand, leading me to
a room within the suite, where there was a worn, leather
armchair facing a mirror. The girl, in broken English, said,
"You must be good friend of Boss Man's to share us." The
girl forced me to sit in the leather chair that was the most
comfortable thing I'd ever sat in. It welcomed my body and
seemed to fit the contour of my back as if it was made for
me. In the background, I could hear Broadway, "Consider
this an early Christmas present." I was having a good time,
but now was questioning the privacy with this woman. She
reappeared with a cold bottle of champagne and a warm
smile on her face, as if she was really enjoying herself. She
was a soft-looking woman with long blonde hair, perfect
C-cup breasts and blue eyes. The shape of her body was
like the ones you would see in "Playboy" magazine, with
the air brush, tight curves, rippled stomach, perfect ass and
toned legs—nothing like this available on the internet, you
betcha. She poured a tall flute of champagne for me and told
me to enjoy her. I was so excited at this point, I resigned
myself that, if I was going to make a sacrifice for this case,
it was definitely going to be with her. I downed the glass of
champagne and started to pour another when I felt the little
blonde tugging on my belt. Leaning back, I let her do with
me what she wanted. She very seductively took my belt off
with her teeth, unzipped my jeans and pulled them out from
under my ass and down around my ankles. I was sitting in
the cool leather seat, looking down at the most beautiful girl
I had ever seen staring at my crotch. She began licking and
biting at my underwear as I stumbled to down another glass
of champagne.

Almost on cue, the speakers in the room started playing a song titled "Alcohol and Ass", perfect for the situation. I put my hands on the girl's face, and she put my fingers in her mouth. At this point, the furthest thing on my mind was police work. I leaned back in the seat, with a strange, warm sensation in the center of my chest, like I just took a big shot of whiskey. I felt extremely buzzed for the amount of alcohol I'd just consumed, but nevertheless totally enjoying the treatment. The young girl slipped her fingers up the side of my boxers and pulled them down, letting out a moan at the sight of my nakedness. While this young girl was pleasuring me, I caught a small clip of the reality of the situation. I thought about stopping, but the sensation of the music, women and booze was too much for me to deny. So I let it happen. After finishing, she got up, wiped her mouth and, with a sweet voice, asked, "You can have more?" I looked up at her and saw double for a second, until the blood returned to my big head. I felt like every muscle fiber, every nerve sensor in my body, was tingling. I pulled my pants up and stumbled out into the main room, where the two other girls were kissing Broadway in tandem. I sat down on the chair, exhausted and watched as they finished him off. Broadway looked at me, winded, and, with a doped smile, said, "How do you like the X treatment?" I was confused, "What's the 'X treatment'?" Broadway, playing with me, responded, "Ecstasy and blowjobs, baby. You can't beat the X treatment." The first glass of champagne that I devoured had a hit of ecstasy in it; I was doped, not drunk. I had never taken any other drug but marijuana when I was in high school, so this feeling was a new one for me. I had gotten a lot of training on the different types of drugs out there, ecstasy being one of them. I remembered they are common club drugs that, combined with alcohol, can give you a euphoric feeling without the limp-dick effect. Thus, they call it the "love drug." Does all this stir some fond or unfond memories, Bro?

Broadway tried one of his games again, which always started with, "What did you say about so-and-so?" I was sure he knew the answer, but—even doped up—I was able to keep my facts straight. By the end of the night, the five of us drank and laughed until the sun came up. The bill was already paid in cash, and I didn't put my hand in my pocket once. Still, I became deeply concerned about how to handle the situation with the drugs. I knew that if it was reported, there would be a chance that I would be pulled from the case. If I kept my mouth shut, chances were I could pass enough time to clean my system out. I used to have dreams about doing drugs and then realizing that I was going to fail my police urinalysis and lose the job—then waking up and being relieved it was a dream. This was like a nightmare come true. The plus side to what was happening is that I bought myself some serious credibility with Broadway. Bro, I'm ashamed of some of the things I've done—things that nobody can ever know about. I have used drugs, slept with whores, accepted unreported money. I did all this in the shadow of trying to do the right thing. The thing is, I've lost sight of what the right thing is. Now, Bro, more totally than ever before. I think you got a sense of this our last night at Hogan's. I was so desperate about things.

Week 5

I feel guilty, but I can't stop. I've been here only over a month, and I'm already dragging my ass. And what do I do? I go to Broadway's "night follies". I go more for the sex—so I can feel good about myself—just for the night. I do, but the next big question has not been addressed. Why hasn't B. given me his business?

Week 6

I've kept away from the "follies" for a week, stressing work problems at Shadow. Still no word.

Then it came. I'd been taking a shower and, when I came out, I found a small, yellow envelope that had been slipped in under the front door. I ripped it open and, in not a very legible handwriting, I read: "Tomorrow night 10 PM, meet me at the gas station at Ponca and Boston," signed "B". I pulled into the Mobile station five minutes before ten, having already called Daddy about the meeting. I had all my surveillance equipment in my car ready to record the event from every angle and my gun stashed so I could get at it quickly if things went south. Clearly this was going to be business or getting murdered.

As I pulled into the lot, I noted a black Escalade parked at one of the pumps. Unsure if that was one of Broadway's guys, I pulled up to the pump just on the other side to check it out. Then I got out of the car, walked around and started the process to pay at the pump—when I heard the sound of an electric window rolling down. I looked around the side of the pump and saw Broadway sitting in the back seat of the truck, looking at me with a smirk on his face, like he'd just cracked a joke about me before rolling the window down. "Frankie, thanks for coming on time, brother. I decided that we need to start negotiating the fee for your services." Feeling like a ton of bricks had been lifted off my shoulders, I smiled. "Sounds good to me, Boss. You want to go somewhere else?" Broadway looked around the empty parking lot. "Naw, go ahead and pump your gas. This won't take long." After being given the instructions, I put the gas nozzle in my car, which was parked in just the perfect spot to record the conversation between the two cars. "OK, Boss, to give you a price, I need to know how big the loads will be." Broadway, without hesitation, "Fifty bricks, every two weeks. You can handle that, right?" I, doing the math in my head, said, "Yeah Yeah, no problem." Trying not to seem like I wasn't capable of giving him accurate figures, I was computing: the average kilo of cocaine costs $17,000 time 50 kilos, that's $850,000 per load and $1.7 million a month. Without hesitation, I blurted out, "125 Gs per load is reasonable for the risk and guaranteed delivery." Broadway looked at his hands, rubbing them together in deep thought, as if he was trying to do the math in his head. "Damn, Frankie, you wasn't kidding about paying for this shit. But if you hold up your end of the bargain on the guarantee thing, it will be worth it in the end." The nozzle popped on the gas pump, and, as I turned around to pull the handle out of the tank, I heard Broadway, "You got yourself some business, Frankie. We'll be in touch." The tinted window rolled up, and the car pulled away from the pump. I put the gas handle back into its cradle and marveled at how I'd just negotiated a $3 million-dollar-a-year drug transportation operation in the time it took to fill my tank. The beauty to the whole thing was that every word between us was recorded and stored as the first piece of evidence in this investigation that just got a huge jumpstart.

After that, I became B.'s master planner, pretending I had already been operating this for "White Shadow". I fine-tuned the scheme, while B.'s parties got wilder. And the cocaine gifts to me more—well, what's the word? M-U-N-F-I-C-E-N-T with each delivery.

Week Eight

Each successful delivery—over a dozen by now—continued to be celebrated by B.'s high-low lifestyle. He sat me next to him. By now, everybody knew Frank Keaton. B. had special vials of coke placed at my feet by the Russian women, each one outdoing themselves in admiration of my feats. Silk suits were ordered to my specifications. Shirts and rings, B.'s chief adornment of self. He tossed me half-sad smiles of the sated emperor, and I ate it up, going from one dizzying high to another, keeping myself fit for the next delivery day, of course.

5 Days Later

We're sitting in the Italian restaurant two days before a delivery was to happen—B., me next to him, Wally (B.'s chauffeur), Latrell to his left and a gaggle of cronies scattered about the room. Latrell keeps looking at me, then away. I can tell, for some reason, he's beginning to lose it. The room's picked up his vibes, and we're all sitting in a tense atmosphere, contrary to the usual conviviality. I've got to talk to Steve. The vinos and the brews hadn't arrived yet.

I felt B.'s hand on my shoulder, then his fingers kneading into me. B. suddenly shouts, "I'm not paying enough heed. There's a knocker out there looking to bring a shitload of trouble. I can feel him. I can't see him, but I can smell him. I told that yo-boy to stop wastin' his time sending toy soldiers here to cross me up! Fuck! The river's full of 'em, but he keeps sending more. After all this time, he should know better. Daddy, my ass! What kind of 'Daddy' do you call that?"

I couldn't believe what he was saying. He'd never once mentioned Daddy before. He stopped working on my shoulder and began muttering to himself. Had Latrell snitched?

"That motherfucker used to be a cousin of mine—when my papa ran the business. Oh, that cousin was no cousin at all! Always at the edge of everything! He wasn't much then, but he was lookin'. He was from the pokey side of the family—very quiet, very sneaky, good manners. Damn! Gailbrait Smith was his name then. His papa was some deadbeat preacher who collapsed while in his pulpit and died. But my papa had a thing for that asshole's ma, by then, a widow person. My papa was too goodhearted. He even thought of putting that boy in the operation. Even talked to him—but that boy had other ideas. Left his mother for a college education. Jesus! None of her tribe was ever wantin' so long as my papa was alive."

The drinks arrived during a deadly silence. B.'s lips moved, but nothing came out of them for the moment. He knocked off the first glass and signaled for more. "Bring the bottle!," he ordered. "Bring all the bottles!"

Daddy is B.'s cousin, Gailbrait Smith! Are you taking this in, John?

Next Night

It wasn't any better. B. seemed even more fixated about the "knocker", but it still wasn't clear who this knocker was. After almost finishing the first Italian-vintage bottle, he wandered back to the subject of yesterday's tirade.

"It's true. It's Gospel—that motherfucker was aimin' to take over once my papa was gone, but he grew to know better. I was set to take over, and here I am. Anybody see anyone but me sittin' here, waitin' for that knocker to show his hand? He'll end up like the others, and Daddy will keep workin' on his revenge for his not being in my place—here—now. But we'll get that white boy, won't we, Frankie?" More testing!

That night, I started on dreaming again. I was back there in the desert, my sights fixed on the dark sand, waiting for the next face to blow to smithereens. As I shot, the faces started changing features. You ready? Daddy's face came up on every other sighting. He rose up to come toward me, and I had to control myself from shooting. I woke up and never got back to sleep—in fear it would go on and on—and I'd shoot!

I was taking B.'s words more seriously than I thought I had. But then I needed to remind myself it was only a dream. Yet how many times before had I repeated to myself those very words—it's only a dream—and found myself taking that extra drink not to be reminded of them. You lose yourself so quickly in dreams that sometimes that extra drink is necessary to believe what you'd like to believe—it's only a dream, Bro. But I wanted to call Daddy—alert him to Broadway's outbursts—yet I hesitated. You see, I wasn't sure whether B. was still testing me or not. I decided to take a chance and called Daddy about B.'s ravings, particularly those about the knocker in our midst. I didn't repeat any of the background stuff If there was a cover agent other than myself here in Pigtown, Daddy needed to know B. was onto him.

I didn't like Daddy's silence before he answered me. "Frank, I am an easy target after all, and your report is not exactly news to me, but I'll look into it, you can be sure."

"Sure"? Right now, I am sure of nothing. In fact, my assignment is getting out of hand. I have to separate the truth from my paranoid thoughts—and the dreams that feed them.

3 Days Later

Christ! I feel like I'm going to kill someone. You fucker! It was you, John, who they wanted to kill. Why the hell didn't anyone tell you? I swear that I'm going to kill Daddy if he didn't tell you about the hit on an unknown knocker—namely you. I finally heard the description of whom they were going to have one of their corner crews murder, and I just knew it was you. And you came damn close to getting killed. That's right, asshole, it was me who killed that piece of shit. John, I can't tell you how screwed-up things are with this case. I can't trust anyone except you, and I know that—if I try to contact you—they will find out. I'm sure that there are cameras in my house, taps on my phone and surveillance crews on me 24-7. All this time, you and I were working the same crew in Pigtown, but in opposite corners, only a body part away—although the blood's the same color at either end.

The Next Day

It was two days to the next delivery, and I decided to lay low. I missed the Broadway "frolics" accordingly, and B. called to know how I was doing and to go over the details of the oncoming delivery. That night, I had an early dinner nearby—alone—and came back for some television and an early night's sleep.

I happened on a rerun of an old Buster Keaton film—one of my favorites. I saw it for the first time at a friend's home when I was fifteen or so. And I found myself doing something I rarely do, that is, to look backwards to the "old days"—not exactly one of my favorite subjects, one that particularly you understood to avoid bringing up in our conversations. But there was no avoiding it now. That little bit about cover names we went over, John—and me coming up with Frank Stevenson, a real smooth-sounding name? The truth was something else—"The Pole with the pole with the unpronounceable name," as you put it. "Polish," you said it was. Like my own real second name—Lithuanian—something that begins with an "M", with all kinds of dots and zeros over letters of that unpronounceable name. How the immigration guys managed to pull "Dixon" out of all those scribble sounds beats me. My sister, Bea, wasn't born yet, but she was the only one who made peace with it. In fact, she was proud of our family and its foreign background. She tried to make my parents appear as a pair of special people. She told me once that they had eloped from the old country. Wow! I've never gotten over that. Whether Bea made it up or not makes no difference. I guess that's about the time I kept imagining that, if my unpronounceable mother and father had really eloped, there must have been someone they were eloping from. Once a man—equally unpronounceable—showed up. I was about three years old. At first, there were all smiles and embraces between the three. Then the visitor—a big man (I remember that) who smelled of garlic—kneeled in front of me, grabbed me and started crying as he babbled in the unpronounceable tongue. I remember my father—a big man himself, who was already half-bald—grabbing this guy by the shoulders and throwing him out of the small apartment we lived in, somewhere in a little town near Rochester. Bea told me the man was my mother's fiancé, but, at the last minute, it was my father she ran off with. I guess I could have been that guy's son, had my mother chosen otherwise. But then what difference would that have made in my life? Maybe a lot more than I can imagine—and I wouldn't be in the situation I am now. The only thing I hated about my assignment was where the action would take place—Pigtown. That name—easily pronounceable—only brought back the image of what my parents slowly, but surely became. "Obese" is the technical term for their condition. I never understood why that happened. Even Bea never could explain it. Something happened between my parents and confirmed my suspicion that eloping was the worst thing that could have happened to them. Later, I heard similar stories about other unpronounceable families in the nabes. They just gave up on one another, on themselves and on the country that was supposed to have solved all their problems, but only did the opposite.

By the time I was ten, my family was on home relief, and I started to feel ashamed of what they'd become. My sister, Bea, was five by then. That she was such a beautiful, happy girl always amazed me. If it wasn't for Bea, I would have run away from home, but she kept me rooted to the old homestead. I kept getting into all kinds of trouble anyway. And when the teacher at public school asked to see my mother, it was Bea who showed up for me—because I asked her. And she did it because we loved each other the way a brother and sister are supposed to. Bea washed and ironed her best little dress and told my teacher that my mother was too ill to come herself. Oh, God, if she had come? My father had learned to speak English in some fashion—my mother categorically refused to on any level. When she went shopping for food, she'd take my sister along to help with money transactions. Once, I had to go with her. On those occasions, I would refer to her as our maid. But everybody knew what the story was by then. I couldn't stand living in the same apartment. They grew more indolent and soon didn't care about anything. As they grew bigger in size, little Bea became the mama. At fifteen, she ran the house, such as it was.

Then I started roaming around. I'd made a lot of friends at school. I was good at everything I did, particularly athletics. I began being invited to the homes of some of these other kids, who lived in nearby neighborhoods, on the border of the area where the unpronounceables had taken up residence. I was shown off as their sons' "best friend" and treated accordingly. All the families spoke English, and I found myself staying with them—sometimes for days, giving some excuse or other about my parents, about whom they knew nothing. I began to enjoy being the "star boarder." I—Frank Dixon. I even received gifts of shirts and other pieces of clothing, but I began to realize that, while I was admired and attended to, their attention had a shade of pity about it. I didn't know how to react to this, except by being more Frank Dixon than ever before. It would be around such times that Bea finally would find me. After school was over for the day, she was waiting by the entrance. She'd take me by the hand when I came out and gently lead me back home, where I belonged. This happened over and over, as I ventured farther afield out of the neighborhood—to find a family that would have me, even for a fleeting time.

Meantime, Bea learned her ABCs on her own, with a little help from me and the library she joined and, later, worked for as an assistant in the Children's Books Department.

It was in junior high that I discovered woodcarving and mechanical drawing workshops. It was in high school that I began to excel in using my wits and hands at many skills. In time, I could install stereo radios in cars, in a garage I worked in after school. And my life began to open up.

Still, Bea would find me—when it was time to "show a little respect for the family." By then, I was fourteen. I was growing up.

My parents passed away—first my father, then my mother. Their hearts gave out on them. There is a picture of us just before that time and one of Bea and myself. I left it in my burn box. Bea found someone at the library, and she was rescued. She married and went to live in Albany.

All during the coming years, we kept in touch—a short visit, a phone call, birthday and Xmas cards. Bea always made sure that, wherever I was, I was alright.
The last time I actually saw her was just before Easter in '03. She'd made me promise that I would join her to visit our parents' graves in Rochester. I marveled at her tears and the prayer she spoke over Mama's and Papa's graves, using occasional unpronounceable phrases that startled me. She was unabashed in her love for those two pathetic people, with their unpronounceable names clearly embossed on their tombstones. Every double-dot and O were there—so long gone, but still alive in Bea's memories, if reluctantly in mine.

One day—that same year, three days before Christmas—Bea was killed in an automobile accident, while going home after work at her library. And there was no more Bea. I never told you about her death—I've been so used to keeping secrets—I just added this one to the others—because that way I kept her still alive.

Why am I writing all this down now, John? I think it's because I'm feeling sorry for myself, and, in my imagination, I can see Bea finding her way here to "take me home" again from the fix I'm in.

What I really meant to do is explain why I took "Keaton" as my cover name (I mentioned Buster Keaton earlier). It was in that old movie of his—where this whole building with an open arch in the middle collapses behind him, but Buster is miraculously framed in the opened arch, so that he escapes any injury, not to mention being killed. That took careful calculation, daring and skill—not to mention courage—bringing it about. One more step to his right or left could have spelled disaster. And, as such things were done in those days, it was a one-time take. I checked up on that.

I felt, going into Pigtown on the most important assignment of my life, that it was important I be at the top of my game—like Buster. One more foot to my left or right could spell the end. That's why I chose "Keaton" as my cover name. It was my secret talisman, to get me through in one piece.

2 Days Later

The delivery was made with no fuck-up, and Broadway was beside himself for such a success. This was his biggest haul so far—and to celebrate it, he had arranged a very special party, to which he invited me and Steve Latrell. It turned out to be a nightmare affair—and a cue for me to make a move.

The party was Broadway's top "frolic"—a lapping party. Fat Randy who ran the shows revealed the deep-seated game Broadway was still playing with me. Broadway said this would represent the perfect indication that, as he put it, "We were perfect asshole buddies—forever." How would

175

I prove that? By an act of degradation! Lapping one of the girls—together—he made an announcement to those masked freaks—that it would be the last item of the evening. I'd been clean on and off and off and on—I couldn't afford even smelling the stuff—I knew me. The big man knew me. So it was sink or swim.

This was evil itself and was B.'s latest attempt to prove my fealty. He is treating me—and will continue to treat me if I let him—like a goat tied to a tree in a lion's den. I made a joke out of it, while I indicated I would do what he requested. You wouldn't have believed the smile that oozed across his drunken lips. I can only describe it as an expression of malevolent pleasure. The slug!

I had no intention of fulfilling my promise. I waited till he was involved in phase one of his freak show until I made my move. I'd chosen the last men's room at the end of the corridor. I'd checked it earlier. It was in such disrepair that B. hadn't even bothered putting surveillance on it. Everything in this place was ancient.
Once inside the john, I locked the door. There was a window above the stalls. I climbed up to the window, praying it wasn't rusted shut like the others. The rusty chain holding the window was frozen in place. There was no way I could move the knobs—they were rusted to a standstill. The window itself was smaller than I figured it to be. The glass was almost obscured by the detritus of a century. I climbed back down, removed my shoes, tied their shoelaces together, and wrapped them 'round my neck. I climbed back up, held one of the shoes by the toe end, and smashed it into the window, which seemed to almost pulverize.

I stopped to listen. No one outside the door came to see what the noise was. I cleared the glass shards around the window frame, and, with my shoes again 'round my neck, I shoved my way out through the frame.

Cars were parked on either side of the window. I looked back down through the now-empty window frame before quickly putting my shoes back on. I moved to my car, ducking down till I found it. I drove back to my apartment, not having been spotted by any of the look-out. Luck was with me. I doubted anything would happen that night, considering the state Broadway was in when I left the "party". By morning, Broadway would know his worst suspicions about me were true. By then, I'd be out of here. So, the wall had fallen down and I'd been standing in the right spot. But there were still problems that I needed to address to get out of this. Against my own will—and measures I took to remain "clean"—I got myself a healthy coke habit that has to be kept away from the unit. I know that, if this case goes to trial, I'm going to have to lie about the coke. Daddy's no doubt going to have to bring it up as an issue in court, and I'm simply going to say that I pretended to take it. I also have about fifty thousand dollars in cash that Daddy has no idea about. I put it in a safe deposit box at the Bank of America in White Marsh under my UC name.

Big PS: My daily reports to Daddy are not going through. Neither are my calls. This happened, I think—although being a little fuzzy, I'm not quite sure it happened—soon after my talk with Daddy about Broadway's ravings over "the knocker" (namely you). I know you're out of Pigtown. Are you back at S.I.S? I'm going into rehab for the coke. I'll be clean and ready to do my part in indicting Mr. Boss Man. I still trust old Daddy to take my side and do the right thing by me when I come out to face the Feds. Meanwhile, I hope that you're OK, pal. I can't wait 'til this is over, and we can go down to Hogan's for some cocktails. I miss my old life. I miss living clean and un-paranoid.
Until I see you, be safe, Bro.

Frank M . . . ôö . . . vic

Yeah!

A FAMILY AFFAIR

Chapter Thirty-Two

I read the diary twice. My immediate response was to pick up the rosary and hold it in the palm of my hand. I stared at the tiny silver image of an untarnished saint that, between the fingers of countless people, represented hope and intercession for salvation.

No doubt Frank retrieved his good luck charm in a desperate lunge for his waning goodness. Toward that end, he was seeking to clean out his habit before attempting to restore his own identity and return to duty at S.I.S. How his brief addiction would be judged by Daddy was yet to be determined. As for Frank himself, he had completed a private journey, leaving behind his many aliases. He had accepted, as "Frank M.", the reality of his own unpronounceable roots. There was no one left for me to intercede for except Marie. It was clear, despite our good intentions, that I was on the verge of losing her—as important, she was on the verge of losing herself. I looked at the icon and thought, "Please don't let that happen!" And then I said it aloud. I put the rosary in the desk drawer and locked it. Locks everywhere—in my case especially, repeatedly keeping love and duty separate from one another, while knowing that the separation had created a toxin that was poisoning our lives.

Here was Frank's diary . . . and his secrets. To show any part of it to Marie would be to show it all. Given its contents, what earthly good would it do her at this moment—when Frank, living and dead, had become a secret enemy in Marie's heart? She never said it, but I knew, I was being forced to a choice—to give up my mission in Frank's behalf or save myself and Marie. Destiny, fate or whatever force had brought me up against the proverbial brick wall.

I could not face the next morning. I wrote a brief note for "My living M".

Forgive me—I know what's happening. I don't want it to happen. I will do everything possible to prevent it. Meanwhile, I can't stand myself. I'm going to try and put my head together. I won't say what you know already. Hell, I will!

J.

I avoided going to S.I.S. I shut down my cell and wandered around Bel Air; but even its autumnal beauty seemed an affront. Trying to concentrate on what my next step was to be, I found myself avoiding that necessity. The day flew by in a haze.

Just about twilight, my cell phone rang once, stopped, then rang again. I'd already piled up a slew of messages, but this one was different. It was the code Marie and I had adopted for ourselves.

"Johnny, where are you?"

"I'm somewhere out in Bel Air."

"I got your note, of course. I won't repeat my tiresome litany of 'understanding', I'm not sure I do anymore."

"Is that what you called to tell me?"

"No, but take it for what it's worth."

"Why did you call?"

"John, I'm at the hospital, and I want you to come . . . right now. There's something you need to see. Come as fast as you can."

"Marie, what is it?"

"OK," she sighed, "it concerns Frank—what else?"

"Frank?"

"You'll see when you get here. Hurry! Go to the back door by the morgue when you arrive." And she hung up.

When I arrived at the morgue, Marie led me to a gurney, on which lay the body of a young man . . . a boy really. The top of his head had been shattered by a high velocity bullet. I looked at the face, wrapped in death, and recognized Kalique.

"There was some shooting heard around Scott Street in Pigtown, and a passerby saw this boy lying in the gutter, and unbelievably, the boy had some life in him. Once he arrived at the ER, he was already dead. We brought him up twenty minutes ago before the police got here." Marie looked pale and frightened, "I want you to see this."

She motioned for me to help roll him over. We turned Kalique's body around. At first, I saw unclear images. Marie pulled over a power lamp and focused it. It was as if we were involved in the making of a horror movie. There were tattoos on Kalique's back. They were in the shape of crude tombstones—two on the shoulders and two below. On three of the tombstones were written three names and dates. It was the third stone, under his right shoulder, that clarified the nature of the horror perpetrated. It read, "Frank Dixon Keaton," and under it a date, "August 25, 2007." In the corner opposite was a large K, like an artist's signature to confirm his accomplishment. Kalique had stolen Frank's wallet to acquire his information. Probably unable to unravel the mystery of Frank's actual identity, Kalique included both names. The same was true of the two other stones—names and dates. The other two implied they, too, might have been undercover men—"Anthony Cirillo" and "Ralph Shaffer". Their deaths were recorded as taking place in 2006, when Kalique was fourteen.

The evidence was incontrovertible—Broadway's child soldiers were also his assassins. And Kalique, his "prince", had been assigned to finish off these "knockers". "Expert knife work," forensics had reported, was Frank's undoing—no doubt learned in early schooling, back in Morocco and wherever the other soldiers had been recruited from. Probably this "talent" was a surety in being accepted for Broadway's army. One had read historically of the Children's Crusade during the medieval siege on Jerusalem. Here was a new wrinkle—a children's army of assassins. Next supposition: Was Kalique's death a result of some private conflict? An attempted robbery, let's say? Or had Kalique been killed by another of B.'s minions? There was too much hanging over Frank—and his involvement in "White Shadow"—to make Kalique's death a random one. Yes—the knife work on Frank had been immaculate.

The telephone call had not been identified as being made by a boy or a man. No matter—Broadway's web of violence most likely provided solutions for every murderous contingency. The fourth tombstone was empty, waiting for the next victim—in this case, Kalique himself. Marie covered up the boy's body.

"We've had so many cases like this lately—children's bodies carrying the emblems of their attacks on others. I don't know what's happening in this city, but I can see them, showing off. Pulling up shirts to display their prizes to one another in a death contest. Like everything else in this city, you try to block it out of your mind—to get on with it. When I saw Frank's name, this time I lost it." She quickly covered Kalique and had the gurney whisked out of sight to the next room.

"What will happen to the boy's body?," I asked tonelessly.

Marie's shoulders slumped in submission to the terrible force dominating life in this city. "There's someone here waiting to ID him."

"Who is it?"

"He says he's the boy's cousin. He looks to be about the same age as . . .," and she pointed off to where the gurney had disappeared. "Where is this cousin?"

"He's been in the waiting room. I wanted you to see what was on . . ."—again she pointed backwards—"before I did anything about the cousin. Don't stick around this place, Johnny. Go home. Wait for me, though."

Marie was so wasted, she sat down in a nearby chair and closed her eyes for a brief respite. I touched her shoulder.

"Johnny, don't stay here. Go back to the apartment and wait up for me."

Chapter Thirty-Three

I recognized the elderly, black nurse at Reception and went over to say hello and all the rest. "Reba, is there a young man in the waiting room?"

"You mean that boy from the Cabbage Patch?" And she wrinkled her nose and lips in distaste.

"Is he still there?"

"Been waitin' since . . .," and she looked at her clipboard. "Since before I went on shift at six. Is he in any trouble? His kind usually is." Reba was itching to add to her list of grievances emanating from the "Cabbage Patch", an area where the poorest of the poor tried to eke out an existence.

I ventured one more question, risking Reba's entrapment, "Is there anyone with him?"

"His is the only name on my list. If there was somebody else, they must have taken off."

"I just want a word with him. Thank you, Reba."

"I'll be here should you need any assistance," she said, her voice tightening in anticipation.

"In that event, I'll be sure to alert you." I made my way down the corridor. The waiting room was the middle one on the right in the corridor marked "Family Area". Usually very active, it was now still. My boot sounded with a rhythmic click on the tile floor. I paused to look through the aperture in the waiting room door, and there he was—Kafir, "Peanut" himself. He had placed three chairs together and was lolling on them, his feet dangling over the edge of the third. He seemed to be concentrating on the ceiling and only moved his head slightly to study me as I approached. He shaded his eyes with his left hand, as if to see me in sharper focus. Then, in a drawl, said, "Hey, man, whatcha doin' here? Lookin' for a taste? Man, it's waaay past my business hours."

"No, I thought we might have another little chat."

"Shit, man." He slouched his way up' till his back rested against the chairs. He lifted his arms behind him to strike a together pose, shut one eye and sized me up with the other. "You're the same one, all right. Sure you are . . . except cleaned up and all that shit."

"'All that shit' is right. And what would you be doing here, my friend?"

"I've been waitin' here to identify my cousin. I've been waitin' here for a long time. You know anything about that?"

"Your cousin is still down in the morgue being examined."

"Examined? What for? You can spot the kid's dead. What else is there to find out?"

"You tell me," I said. And he rose up.

I pressed my thumb against his chest and poked him back on to the chair. He looked up at me with utter surprise, then shifted his head sideways.

"Are you up to doin' an investigation sort of thing?"

"I've always asked you questions, Peanut, and you've always been most obliging." Peanut hunkered downward, looked toward the doorway, while considering his options.

"Shit man, I never been investigated before. You said 'chat', man."

"Exactly," trying to put him at ease by using the familiar word.

He laughed a boyish bleat of a thing. There was a note of excitement in it, as if "chatting" with a now-recognized officer of the law, a knocker, in fact, opened some private urge, even need in him, to do so. He looked at me coyly again, not a typical Peanut expression.

"I was home eatin' my supper, when I got this call to go to the hospital because my cousin's body was there."

"Who called you?"

"Leon."

"Who's Leon?"

"He was workin' next to where my cousin was workin'. He picked up the news and told me to come here to see if my cousin was alright. Gamma couldn't do it, so it was up to me. Who else?"

"Who's 'Gamma'? I heard your cousin mention that name."

"Gamma is his grandma. He's got no mamma . . . except his Gamma."

"Then why didn't she come to the hospital?"

"What's wrong with me doin' it?" He removed his arms from the chairs in a quick, confrontational move.

"You're a minor. Can't let you make decisions."

"'Minor.' How do you mean that?"

"You're seventeen. The hospital won't take responsibility."

"Sure, I'm seventeen," he interrupted. "And what's wrong with being seventeen?!"

"Look, I don't want to play games with you."

"I'm not playing games. I'm the onliest one of the family who could do it. Gamma don't speak no English. And besides that, she'd try to put one of those spells of hers on the whole friggin' place, and then what?" Peanut relaxed again and started adjusting his crotch. "Sure, I'm seventeen—and I'm the head of the family. Who else but me?"

"Exactly—who else but you?"

"You don't have to repeat that for my sake. I know that already."

"And I know that, too." I decided to tag along with his nonsense games to see how long it would take to get what I wanted from him.

"You're bein' smart with me, man," and he tilted his head in a gesture to blow off my authority here on the edge of Pigtown. "Now why you doin' that? I'm tellin' the truth, and you're funnin' with me."

"OK, what about that day?"

"Which day?"

"The day after our last little chat. The day I was almost killed."

"I had nothin' to do with that!"

"How about your cousin, then?"

"He had nothin' to do with it either."

"Then who did?"

"Believe me, man, I'm not sure. There was a lot of talk passing 'round the streets about my lookin' at the bottoms of your shoes. And, all of a sudden, we had this shift change, and the next thing, the monkey's dead."

"What monkey?"

"The 'monkey,' man. The salesman who works with me."

"Then who killed Kalique?"

"OK, that's easy. I did."

"You?"

"I had my orders."

"You killed your own cousin?"

"Better me than anybody else. I had no hate in my heart and no room on me to have to fill in."

"What 'room'? What are you talking about?"

And without a moment's hesitation, Peanut stood up and slowly removed his shirt; then, just as methodically, his shoes and trousers. He piled them neatly on the chairs, then turned 'round to face me. Peanut's entire body, from his upper torso to his toes, was obscured with tattoos of different sizes and configurations—animal heads, serpents, wild geometric designs, fantasy faces, the sun, yes, even tombstones, spider webs, outsized flowers. I stopped looking. Every item embossed on his naked body was identified, dated and initialed. Peanut was a walking cemetery. Kalique's four tattoos were a mere drop in the assassin's bucket. But not all parts of Peanut's torso were so endowed. He was wearing a pair of boxer shorts. And he dropped those—then turned around—his butt cheeks were crowded with weapon tattoos. Then he turned back front.

"That's my love spot," he said and did his little bump again. "That doesn't have anything on it. That's sacred territory, man, or don't you believe me?" He posed full frontal demonstrating a truly oversized penis—he caught my look—"That's why they call me Peanut—You get it," and he laughed.

"I thought since we were still chattin', I could let you know everything I could."

"Are the initials . . . are they of white men?"

"White men people of my own color, and some women, too. I stopped countin' them."

"You . . . killed them . . . all?"

"That's part of my job. When I get my orders, I do what I'm told to do."

"How many on there were knockers?"

Peanut spread his arms wide and came forward, the slowly gyrated his body—for my closer inspection. "I don't recall the numbers, but their initials and dates are all over the place."

"What about Kalique? Why him?"

He stopped circling, "Like I told you, he's my cousin, but he talks too much. There was a big job, and I didn't have it on me to get it done myself. So Kalique offered. He did a good job, but he kept runnin' his mouth about it all over town and Abu didn't like that. He likes things done his way, and Kalique kept tellin' everybody what he'd done about takin' out a cop. The little dumbass even got the full name of the dude tatted on his back instead of the initials like everyone else."

"So it was Abu who asked you to . . . ?

"Abu loved my cousin. Abu loves all of us—but if you cross him . . ." Peanut shook his head.

"And you did it as a favor?"

"He knew I would do it right—quick—no meanness to it. Not like the others—And there was no need to take credit. Everybody knew."

"So you did it quick? Not like the others?" And I pointed to his body.

"If what they did deserved it—otherwise it was," and Peanut sighed. "Besides, it's all over now that I'm retired." He ran his fingers lightly over his body. "I don't need to do nothin' but sell."

"There you go again—retiring. Retiring from killing, you mean?"

"Man, there's no more room on me to put a new date or new initials on. When that happens, you stop. That's the rules in Pigtown, and you retire."

"I see. Retire to where?

"I get a brand-new car of my own choice, an apartment—and a percentage of what I'm takin' in off the street. I'm the onliest one to retire in five years now. The others tried to keep up with me—and each other—but they're way behind," and he glowed with pride. "That's why I didn't finish you off."

A hot sting of anger shot threw me, "And what about me?"

"No room," crouching his body for me to see the endless ink on his body. "That's why the monkey got the job, to help fill his quota." Then he chuckled in a psychotic way.

He began to put his clothes back on. "That's it, yo. Lunchtime's over."

With a little shrug, Peanut started toward the exit. I grabbed him by his shirt front, swung him around and pushed him up against the wall. He looked at me now with the hard, gloating expression of a pure thug.

"Are you thinkin' of throwin' me in the lock-up? Hey, man, you know that won't do any good. Initials are just initials. You said it yourself—I'm a minor, not to mention certified bi-polar. Bossman has got these lawyer types who look out for our welfare. No matter what, man, I'm too important to Abu, man, for you to try fuckin' me over, Motherfucker," and he spat in my face with full force. I punched him squarely on the chin and left him on the floor, unconscious, wrapped in his obscene souvenirs.

"And he was right, Marie. He was right. To arrest him would be to arrest a long chain of similar offenders, all hell-bent to do their duty by Broadway. I've never felt so completely helpless in my life . . . to do my duty."

"Reba found the boy on the floor," Marie said. "Did you hit him?"

"I did. He pushed me too far."

We were back in our apartment, now sharing a moment of silence while we drank our late-night coffee. Marie had listened in a composed frame of mind. A little color had returned to her cheeks. She rose, put her empty cup in the sink, and returned to sit opposite me. She looked me over, shut her eyes a moment, then spoke very calmly.

"Johnny, I just want you to know that I've handed in my resignation at the hospital. I've got to get away from this place, and I need to get away from you. Tonight, with that dead boy—and his cousin—not the least all this stuff with Frank . . . It's just that I can't go on living as we are. Please, please don't say anything until I finish. You've had your say. You guys keep talking about catching a case of the 'blues'. Well, I've caught a case as blue as my scrubs. Like living here, with all of Frank's clothes in our closets? I've accepted that he's gone, but, Johnny, you keep holding onto him. And part of it I truly understand, but the other part of it is that I don't want to understand any longer. Can you understand that? I feel pushed away—by all those clothes and all the baggage connected to them and that boy passed out on the floor. There's something you've got to do about all of it—something only you can do, for your sake. And when you've done it, call me. I'll be back in Massachusetts. Call and tell me my closets are clear of everything but our own things. If that sounds like a warning, take it as such. I love you too much not to make it sound that way. Otherwise, we'll be swallowed up in this thing. And, destiny or not, there's no chance for us, Johnny. No chance at all. If you believe what you read and see, Baltimore is not just Baltimore anymore. There are Baltimores all over this country—all over this world—places going to hell. If that happens, I'd like to know there's someone by my side to help me bear it, and I'd like it to be you. I'll always love you, but I don't want you to be some sweet memory. I want you with me." She looked straight at me, waiting for my response.

I'd listened to Marie quietly. I'd already been developing my plan of action. All the evidence was now in, and it spoke loud and clear. As to what would be next—

"I'll be there," I said. "Wherever it is you'll be, I'll be there."

Five Days Later

Marie left for Massachusetts this morning. I drove her to the train station, promising to call. When I returned to the apartment, I found a note from Marjorie Wyatt in the mail. I immediately thought of her tattoos, harmless love tokens as compared to Kalique's death notices. Marjorie's tattoos formed a circuitous link to Frank's death. Hers will disappear under an expert's handiwork. Kalique's taking them to his own grave. Peanut's will remain mordant souvenirs in "retirement", until it's his turn to face the inevitable.

I was holding Marjorie's note as I thought this—a thank-you note for the white summer dress I'd returned to her by mail. The old world of thank-you notes lay so far behind me. Along with the note, there was a photo of Marjorie with her family—father, mother, sister and the dentist brother. The faces of these good people were part of my growing up. I quietly thanked Marjorie for reminding me such a world still existed. Thinking of my own parents, I wondered what they would make of my next "adventure", as they put it. I determined to call them this evening around dinnertime.

Do you send a thank-you note in return for a thank-you note? I must ask my mother.

FREE WILL

Chapter Thirty-Four

"And the reason, John?"

"I think this period of stress leave has managed not to alleviate the condition, but actually to aggravate it, sir."

Daddy looked at me from behind his shades and nodded solemnly.

"I do have vacation time coming to me, and right now I'd welcome a couple of weeks by myself."

"What about your girlfriend . . . Marie?"

"She's taking time off to attend to her ailing mother in Massachusetts."

"Is that all there is to it?"

"We've been on each other's nerves with all that's happened, and . . . need I say it, sir?"

"No. Of course you can have your leave, John. And, on your return, we can orbit you back into Operation White Shadow."

"Oh?"

"The court proceedings are already underway. Your input will be crucial. Have you any idea where you'll be going?"

"I've made some inquiries. Maybe even visit my own folks up North. I haven't seen them for quite some time."

"Three weeks. Is that it?"

"Yes, sir. And, sir, the clothing matter has already been taken care of."

"When?"

"Two days ago. I consigned the bulk of Frank's clothes to the Salvation Army. And that's it."

"Good going, son."

"I finally took to heart what you said about . . . holding onto old memories."

"I knew you would." And he crinkled his mouth in a self-satisfied grin.

"I thought—as a final homage to our friendship—I'd complete the closure process on Frank's birthday."

"In what way?" The grin disappeared.

"The burn box, sir. I'm afraid I have malingered in that respect. I ask your final indulgence—it will be put to the fire that day."

"A ritual act, I take it, John? But then, given your relationship, very apt." And his shoulders slumped forward in a tangible sign of relief.

"Anything else, sir?"

"No, not really. Except I'm sorry you will be missing all the fun."

"Fun? Under the circumstances at S.I.S, what possible 'fun' could I be missing?"

"I meant that, hypothetically. Any man's ruin—friend or foe—is a lamentable thing. But we're anticipating that Randy will succeed with Broadway, and there will be a lot of accounting for in the D.C. political circles. I'm sorry you might not be here once that aspect of the case goes into action."

"In any event, you know where to reach me . . . in case you get curious." And Daddy shook my hand.

"I look forward to your return, John."

"Thank you, sir, and good luck as far as Randy is concerned."

"I think it's going to fall our way. I really do," Daddy said as he walked me to the door.

It had all been accomplished quite easily—phase one, that is. Perhaps too easily. Whatever else Daddy might be holding up his sleeves, to clarify his use of the word "fun" would be managed by him in his inscrutable way. Right now, I couldn't give a good fuck!

Chapter Thirty-Five

From then on, things happened serendipitously. I rented a Nissan SUV, then drove to the post office in the next county. On the walls were the usual cards and notices offering short-term rentals. My eye found it almost immediately: "A small furnished house outside Baltimore." Available for two months as of October 21. A pick-up truck went with it. "Please call."

The voice that responded was congenial, sounded to be around my age and relieved to find a taker. The price was amenable. I gave him a general identification as an officer with the Baltimore Police. He was a bachelor working for the local AT&T branch, as a contractor managing local sales. My insistence on paying cash closed the deal. I could begin occupancy in two days.

What I was contemplating doing was a brutal thing. Brutality is not in my second nature. Not even my third. There was simply a compelling urge to savor this streak, searching in myself for my soul's fault. Like a land fault that, under continued pressure in nature, could wreak havoc. I understood this premise to exist in us all. I'd experienced its twinge on the street. A residue of some unresolved rage already present in us, its source not always possible to pinpoint. It was just there—haunting our imaginations—and necessary to rationalize away in the course of our daily lives. We sought private outlets to covertly introduce it into some part of our lives. I can recall from my college days, and for years after, the special thrill there was in hunting down animals—especially deer—at some point—even bears. These adventures gave cognition to the 'fault'—accepting it as permissible in the form of sport—an activity capable of drawing blood. I had not anticipated this turn of thought while contemplating Broadway's end. Sport? Hardly. But the blood? The thought of that eventuality would not easily go away. Certainly while in Pigtown it began to subtly insinuate itself. My little rental was nowhere near Maryland's hunting grounds where I had exercised my "sport" in congenial company; Frank was not part of that company. Blood sport had no interest for him. Here I was now, caught up in the reverie of those times. I had purposefully brought the equipment that would be needed if a hunt were to present itself.

There is no better time to think and reflect on life than sitting in a deer hunting stand, waiting for that big buck. A good hunter knows how to look and listen to the woods, but more importantly learns how to use his mind as the only thing moving to pass time. I looked forward to sitting in a tree stand for more than eight hours, not moving a muscle, alone, thinking about everything under the son. It's like meditation that has the potential to end with the crack of a rifle or wisp of an arrow.

It was mid bow and arrow season in Maryland, the leaves were turning and the deer were in their pre-rut patterns. Although Operation White Shadow had taken up so much time, I still had permission to hunt an old farm in Fallston where a stand had been permanently built into a tree. That stand was like a good fishing hole; you could keep going back to it year after year, and it consistently produced.

My alarm was set for 4:00 am. I had a ritual that I followed before a morning hunt. I started with a hot shower, making sure that I washed my entire body thoroughly with a scentless soap. A deer can smell a sweaty armpit or crotch hundreds of yards away; keeping my scent to a minimum would allow me to get close. After showering, I had to put a cup of coffee and a few breakfast bars in my stomach—nothing worse than stomach growls on stand. I also had to prepare all my equipment, make sure that batteries were fresh and a gutting kit with paper towels, rubber gloves and water were handy. The final preparation was sharpening the Gerber knife set that Marie bought for me when we first met. I learned the hard way many times before to check each piece of equipment and replace the batteries that had been in storage since the year before. There is nothing worse than getting halfway to your stand in total darkness to have your flashlight die, or have to take a shit with no toilet paper on hand. A good hunter learns from his mistakes and prepares better in the future.

Clothing selection is always a guess, as temperatures change in the woods and it's hard to determine so early in the morning whether you need to bundle up or dress light. As part of my ritual, I stuck my head out the front door and blew a strong breath into the dark air. If there was breath vapor, wear a jacket; if not, wear a pull-over. This morning there was a hard crisp white cloud that made the guess work easy. As part of my scent control, I kept all my hunting clothes in a sealed plastic bin that contained dirt scent wafers. It's a marinade of sorts for clothes to become invisible to their keen noses. I dressed in layers, making sure that each layer was tucked into the next. I decided to wear my fall foliage 3-D camouflage jacket and matching coveralls. I tucked a like camouflage scent-lock balaclava to cover my head and face into my jacket pocket; I would dawn it once on stand. To a deer looking directly at me, I would look more like a tree than anything. The final preparation was to check my weapon. I unsnapped the latches from my bow case and opened it to find the bow, arrows, trigger release and quiver just as I had left it the year before. I pulled the velcro straps from the bow off and pulled it out of the case, inspecting the string to make sure it wasn't too dry. Just for good measure I rubbed a wax stick along its strands and pulled it back to a fire position with ease. The hunting tips were already fixed to the arrows; I gave each one a quick check to make sure they were tight. I packaged the bow back up and left the house with a good feeling about my preparation and chances for a successful hunt.

I always parked in the same place on this property so the owner knew it was me on the premises. I had to drive at least a half mile down the hedgerows and cornfields to get to my spot. I got into the stand without any problems, stowed my gear on a hook that I screwed into the tree and knocked an arrow in the bow. I sat there motionless in the dark, waiting for the sun to break the horizon, listening to the sound of my own breath. I instantly felt at home and relaxed for the first time in a long while. The woods slowly showed itself as the sun came up and the temperature dipped for that hour as the sunlight heated the cool earth. This was my favorite time on the stand; it was also the best shot at getting a deer since they are nocturnal and still moving about the woods freely. I always referred to the time just after the sun comes up and goes down as the "hunting hour".

There is a distinctive sound that separates deer walking through leaves from the normal sounds of squirrels and birds scurrying around. The rustling leaf sounds are slower than any other animal, more consistent and deeper. My ears informed me of this approaching sound behind me, moving in my direction. The sounds got louder, and I could tell there were at least two deer. They didn't seem to be spooked, but they walked through the woods cautiously. I looked at the leaves on the trees in front of me slowly billowing away from me, which was a good indication my scent was not blowing in their direction.

My heart started pounding in my chest as the sounds were so close, I couldn't believe that I didn't see movement yet. I was afraid to move anything other than my eyes at this point, as deer can pick unnatural movement out very well and I didn't want to blow it. Through a crack in the stands floorboards, I caught the flicker of a brown ear directly under the tree stand. Deer rarely look up unless they detect unnatural sounds or movement; they tend to look ground level out in front of them. I took this opportunity to stand up and attach my bow string release trigger. I was skilled at moving without sound and putting myself into position before a kill. I always felt comfort in the adrenalin-fueled rush of knowing that life was hanging on each second. The two deer moved out in front of the stand still facing away from me, unaware that a killer was less than twenty yards away. I picked out the buck right away, counted six points and focused on his movements to calculate the exact time to draw and shoot. The stand was positioned at the intersection of four corn fields; a stream ran through the middle, which was a large patch of woods. The two deer changed directions and started heading toward the stream bank that put them in perfect broad side position for a shot. I waited until the target's head was hidden by a tree, and I silently drew the bow, taking the pin sights into view. The buck continued moving on his course as I let out a faint buck grunt, "Whuurp!" He froze in his tracks and looked in my direction, I placed my twenty yard sight pin just below his heart and gently eased on the trigger release. The arrow shot away quietly and passed directly through his side coming to rest in the dirt on the other side of where he was standing. The two ran off in tandem into a thicket of brush leading into a corn field. Having killed many deer before with bow and arrow, cartridge rifle and black powder, I knew that deer with a heart and lungs split in two can run out of sight as if never touched. This was nature's way of showing that adrenalin and will to survive can suppress certain death for a short amount of time.

After waiting a few moments, I got out of the stand with all my equipment, knocked another arrow and quietly moved to where the arrow was sticking out of the ground. I pulled the arrow out of the dirt; it was covered from end to end in bright red slime, indicative of a perfect double lung shot. You can often tell if the shot was fatal by the color of blood on the arrow. Red means it's dead within a short radius, brown means you got a gut shot ad could potentially never find the deer. The next step is to pick up a blood trail and slowly, methodically track it to the carcass.

I use a special kind of arrow head that opens up upon impact with three two-inch blades. These razor-sharp tips allow for a four-inch exit wound that helps keep the blood loss going and makes it easier to track. This case was no different; right from the shot point, there were heavy bright red, oxygen-filled blood drops covering the pre-fall foliage. I moved slowly through the brush following the trail into the corn. I zigzagged, following the blood smears on the corn stalks, knowing that I was closing in as the pools of blood got larger and darker. There is nothing more primal than this. I heard a sudden struggle in front of me and saw a group of corn stalks tip over as if something had been laid on them. I quickly moved to the motion and saw the wounded deer gasping for breath, kicking its legs into the dirt in an effort to use every piece of energy to escape death. I drew my final arrow and put it surgically through his throat into the brain causing instant death. His chest took a final breath of air, the legs stiffened, and then he was still.

I sat down in the dirt, heart still pounding with adrenalin and realized that I felt no remorse. I had no feelings of regret or sorrow for taking life in such a savage way. It empowered me; I realized that I liked killing and even understood it was nature's way of thinning the herd, and the Baltimore streets had widened the dark fault in my soul.

I then prepared the deer to be dragged out of the woods and taken home for butchering in the garage. I realized that in all the concentration of tracking and killing, the corn maze had turned me around. I knew that the path to get back to the car was well out of the way, so I used my Garmin hand held GPS to give me the straightest line back. A wrong turn in these three hundred plus acre fields could put you wandering around for miles. I always carried a GPS unit in the woods and kept waypoint markers programmed to get me home.

Once I got back to the house, I strung the deer up neck first in the garage and put some plastic down to catch the drippings. I always butchered my own deer and used an old Amish secret to getting the blood and game flavor out of the meat. I prepared a bucket filled with ice, water and salt. As I took the cuts of meat off the carcass, I placed them into the cold salty water, where the blood vessels would contract, pushing out the blood and adrenaline that makes the meat taste strong. I cracked open a beer and opened up the knife set to start butchering.

First things first—I needed to cut the hide away from the meat. I learned from so many deer before this one that you only need to get a cut started a few inches around the edges. Once you got enough hide away from the muscle and bone, you could pull it down without having to make cuts. I wondered if human skin would separate from the muscles and bone like this, if pulled. Once the hide was pulled to the floor like a crumpled pair of pants, the large carcass was nothing but flesh and bone. I sat down on the stairs into the house to catch my breath since I was holding it for some reason when pulling the skin off. I took a large gulp from my beer and belched.

All the training I'd had with a knife that I got in the past was with rubber training knives; I never actually practiced the techniques into real flesh and bone, but I would imagine it wasn't as easy as plunging a blade into tissue trying to avoid bones. As if challenged by that fact, I stood up, took the attack stance and lunged at the carcass, plunging the hunting blade repeatedly into the side of the neck, throat and ribs. I remembered that strategically placed cuts to the neck, liver, kidneys and main artery points would render a person dead before they knew they were mortally wounded. With each cut, I felt the uncontrollable rage and struggle within me to resist the temptation of re-enacting this carnage on Broadway. I had descended into a place within my soul that harbored a killer's thoughts. But even as I thought this, I felt as if I had been part of something larger, larger than my single self. It belonged in mythology where animal sacrifice to the gods was part of accepting the totality of life itself—where the sacrifice was made to ward off the darkness of evil sendings, to help the spirit of hope and goodness shirk off its back all that threatened it. Daddy had used the word ritual in connection with my tribute to Frank on November 12. What was to happen—all that would happen—would be an inextricable part of that ritual.

Just like Fat Randy and Latrell in the interview room, I was now at that crossroads of life. I knew that killing Broadway would change me forever, but I also knew that by not doing anything, I would carry guilt with me like Frank's haunting spirit.

Chapter Thirty-Six

While working undercover in Pigtown, I'd kept a part of me alert to Broadway's own movements. I'd already memorized the license plate numbers of several cars he had been spotted in—driving or being driven—hoping to learn where the Boss Man mostly lay his head down at night.

Now, months later, here I was driving the small pick-up truck that came with the rental, on the same mission. This time, I'd changed the truck's license plate. I would continue to follow him, tracking down his activities. I'd follow him for hours, which became very difficult, due to the frequent stops he often made.

I noticed a pattern that Broadway was making just to make phone calls. Broadway was a king at the game and knew that you never talk on a cell phone—they're too easy to tap. Broadway would randomly find payphones every hour throughout the city and county to contact his people. This practice was smart—he would never get caught on tape by taking this precaution.

I followed Broadway at great risk to being spotted. People like Broadway often used counter-surveillance techniques, such as taking three right-hand turns, to see if any cars were following. The first time he did this, I almost got caught. The second time, I repositioned to pick him up at an intersection where he started from. After several hours of this, Broadway called it quits and drove to his house—the one that nobody knows about, but he calls home.

The house was nestled away in a remote, country section of Baltimore County, about twenty minutes north of the city—thirty from my rental. The city thugs were getting smart about where to lay their heads. The county was safer. The police gave a shit, and the neighbors wouldn't tolerate criminal activity. I identified the house and left the area. I had what I needed and felt that any more pressure might blow my cover.

For several days, I drove by the house early in the morning to make sure that Broadway's car was parked outside and that it wasn't just one of his stash houses. On one of my early morning drive-bys, I had the opportunity to pick up the trash that was left at the end of the driveway. Trash is a great tool to find out what's going on inside of a house. You can often determine if there are males and females, how old they are, what their names are, if they're using the house to cut and bag up dope and even what their favorite foods are.

I found, inside the trash, a lot of good intel that would help me eliminate Broadway without leaving a trace. I learned that there were three people living inside the house—Broadway, a female named Lakesha Brown and a young male child still in diapers. There were a number of Newport-brand cigarette butts and the innards of Philly blunt cigars. Broadway used the cigar wrappers to smoke marijuana. There were also empty wine bottles and a set of used rubber gloves. I took the gloves found in the trash, turned them inside out, and placed them in a Ziploc bag. By turning the gloves inside out, they could be used to leave behind another set of prints, if needed.

I also had to figure out what method I was going to use to assassinate Broadway. The good thing I had going for me was the fact that there was a long list of people that wanted to kill him. When the majority of these thugs get killed, it's usually labeled "drug-related". That means the death was a result of his dealings in the game, and—in that Darwin-style environment—it's a matter of time before you get got. It was also a plus that Broadway's house was in the county. There would no doubt be a homicide investigation, and the fact that he's a city thug would make it that much tougher for them to get information. The city Homicide Unit is so overworked and understaffed that any help out of them would be unlikely. An unsolved murder of a city drug dealer would be viewed as a warning to other drug dealers that you're not safe anywhere. For Frank's sake and for my other fallen brothers and the evil abuse of innocent children, I wanted to give Broadway a painful death—not a Peanut quick, lights-out style, like a gun or a car bomb, but the kind of death that lets him feel the life pumping out of his body and the overwhelming fear and anticipation of the end. It was also clear that I had to do it up close and personal, so that Broadway, in the end, would know who killed him. It had to be done with a blade and the image of my savage attack on the suspended deer of memory flashed through my head.

I had attended a week-long training course several years prior called, "The Use of Tactical Edged Weapons as a Last Resort". The purpose of this course was to teach law enforcement and military operators how to use an edged weapon when all else failed. It was Classroom 101 on how to kill, maim, etc., all with a knife.

I found that B. often left his house at approximately 10 am. The girl and the kid would leave earlier in the morning, before Broadway, which gave me a good window of opportunity to be alone with him and ensure no witnesses. To be safe, I would park my vehicle a half-mile away on a dirt service road and walk through the woods to the back of Broadway's house. This would be done in the dark so that, when the sun came up, I would already be in place. There were hopefully not going to be any gunshots to alarm the neighbors who would summon the police and if the cuts were deep and accurate, there wouldn't be any screams. Just in case though, I had an untraceable .40 cal strapped to my hip.

In some deep part of me, I felt Frank urging me to use the Kershaw in his burn box. I knew then it would serve a higher purpose. I even stashed a loaded M-4 assault rifle just inside the tree line in case I had to fight my way out of there. So I removed it from the box, and I took the time to sharpen the knife to a point that, when I scraped my fingers across the side of the blade, it would cause the hair to stand up on the back of my neck. I was also very cautious of trace evidence. A small drop of Broadway's blood on any part of my body and clothes would be enough to link me to the crime scene. Therefore, any clothing I wore had to be burned, along with any other evidence that could work against me.

November 12th, one week later, I woke up at 4 am and began preparation for the main event. I put my clothes on as if my life depended on it. One screw-up—one little molecule of my DNA left behind—could end it all. I wore, under my clothes, pantyhose on my legs, arms, and head to help seal any possibility that hair would be left at the scene. I laced up my size 10½ boots, which I purposely bought two sizes too big to throw off any footprints left behind.

It took approximately twenty-five minutes to reach the service road from my house. From there, I fired up my handheld GPS and began slowly stalking through the dark forest toward Broadway's house. I had twenty minutes to move one-half mile until the sun would be up and I would need to be in place to execute my plan.

As I spotted the house, I could see the lights on in the upstairs bathroom, where Broadway's girlfriend was doing her normal, everyday routine. I also knew that within the next fifteen minutes, she was going to leave the house for work, and I could then move into my final position. Like clockwork, the girl left the house with the boy, got into their vehicle and pulled out of the driveway. After several minutes, I decided to move along the wood line and into the position I'd picked out on the side of the house. It was a good spot to stay out of sight from the neighbors and on the opposite side of the driveway. When Broadway would leave the house, he would be focusing on his vehicle and have his back to where I would be waiting with blade in hand. As I slipped into position, my heart started pounding inside my shirt. It was a feeling that I'd learned to embrace—fear. It was also the most primal kind of fear, the kind that brewed inside my soul for years, while policing the most violent streets in the country. I had last felt it in Pigtown—faced by my would-be assassin's gun.

I looked around Broadway's property and found myself praising the fastidious side of his nature. November's leaves and stray branches had been cleared—that might have given my approach away.

I heard the sound of Broadway's 250-pound frame moving around in the foyer at the front door and the sound of keys being picked up. It was game time. My thoughts began to become irrational. I thought about the fact that Broadway had no clue that he was seconds away from dying. I moved to the corner of the house and used a tactical position called the "Israeli sweep" or "slicing the pie". Essentially, it's positioning yourself at a corner where you can see what or who is around the corner, but he can't see you.

The front door opened. Then the creek of the screen door. Then the thump of the main door closing. I could see the rear heels of Broadway's Timberland boots as he turned around to lock the deadbolt with his key. Broadway then turned away and began walking off the one-step porch to the path leading to the driveway. I had played this moment a million times over in my head. I had to make my move when Broadway took at least two steps off the porch. I could tell that Broadway's guard was down and that his street-survival skills were on hold when he was in his country home. I had also calculated the time and place to minimize approach noise.

It was time. I slowly moved out of my fixed position, walking on the palms of my feet to minimize noise, my blade fixed in my hand. My heart was beating so loudly that it was the only thing I could hear, and I feared it was so loud that Broadway, only feet away, would hear it, too. As I approached him from behind, I raised my blade to the level of Broadway's neck. I was about to make my first contact. The primal instinct that we all have kicked in, and Broadway sunk his neck down, raising his shoulders, unaware of what was about to attack him. I moved to Broadway's right and slammed the blade into the side of his neck, just under his jaw. In a quick, sawing motion, I brought the blade out the front of Broadway's neck. I knew that the wound I'd inflicted was fatal, painful and every bit of what he deserved. Broadway fell onto his back as I stood over him. The sound of air escaping his lungs through his severed windpipe covered by a fountain of blood spilling out of a pierced artery made for a horrific gurgling sound. Broadway just stared at me in disbelief that he was going to die. I bent down in front of Broadway and calmly said, "Hell is waiting."

And, unexpectedly, the manner of Frank's death, as I imagined it, kicked in, and I followed that formal design as Broadway rolled over in an effort to escape. I plunged the blade into his lower spine, twisting the handle back. As I did so, Broadway's body went limp. I stood over him and with my left hand raised his head for a last glimpse of his face. I slashed his windpipe open even wider, almost severing his head from his shoulders. The formal ceremony was completed. The vision faded.

Abu Boss Man's huge frame twitched spasmodically on the ground. His fingers splayed, trying to find a grip on the earth that would soon cover him. The pupils of his eyes lost focus and shriveled as the lights went out of them. Some final stench of self emanated from him, and he was still. The gurgling sound erupted in a final spasm. Before I hit the tree line in my escape from the area, Broadway had bled out in the driveway in front of his car where no one would see him if they drove by.

As I approached the truck, I had already removed my gloves and jacket. They were placed into a garbage bag and tossed in the back of the truck. I left the service road, making sure that I obscured my face from any passing vehicles for miles until reaching the next county. I'd scouted out a small burn pit at a vacant campsite that was secluded and never used during the week. The clothes, the socks, the pantyhose, the paper temp tags—everything that would burn, even the knife that was covered in Broadway's blood—were set ablaze. I sat and watched the flames and thought about my childhood barbecues on the beach, thinking about how much I'd changed over the years. After the fire dimmed and there was nothing left but ash, I fished the knife out of the fire that was cleansed of any usable DNA and placed it in a cardboard box.

I made a new fire for the last item—the burn box. I decided to burn it entirely, in one piece, not to suffer it item by item. I thought of Frank inside, still holding the severed head into eternity. As Egypt's sphinx-and-palm setting curled into nothingness, the monument's wise smile seemed an appropriate epithet. I put the ashes in a separate bag, which I took with me. I kept Frank's journal—I had many reasons to do so.

The next stop was the carwash, to make sure that the outside of the truck was thoroughly rinsed of any potential trace evidence.

My last stop was the wooded area under the Hanover Street Bridge, where I threw the burn box ashes into the river and, finally, hurled the Kershaw knife as far as I could throw it. The surface was calm, and the meager plop that resulted could have been a fish, briefly surfacing, then disappearing.

Chapter Thirty-Seven

Back at my rental, I took the longest shower I'd ever taken—as if my body was visibly stamped, gouge and deformed by Pigtown. I was spewing its shit down into the small drain in the smallest room in this small house that had been my refuge and hideout. As if I was palpably able to touch these scars, I scrubbed and rescrubbed my torso. There was no limb, no orifice so sacred (as in Peanut's case) that was not tainted. Three, four, five times—each part scrubbed until I was satisfied the toxins had given in.

I felt no guilt for what I'd done. I was as much a soldier as any of my mates in a deserted army, forced to eliminate the enemy while forging for personal safety. I thought of the rosary and realized I'd unconsciously interceded for myself—to reclaim my goodness in a world seemingly disinterested in such commodities. It was an act of personal preservation against Broadway's wanton evil. When at war, the enemy is the enemy. My Pigtown assignment had been enforced and properly closed.

I stood dripping wet in front of a large mirror over the fireplace in the living room. All I could do was laugh and dry—laugh and dry. If I'd had a camera handy, I'd have taken a latter-day baby picture of myself and kept it as a souvenir. The photo would be a stunner on Hogan's wall.

That night, I called Marie. I had two propositions in mind—one concerning her, the other myself, and both inevitably intertwined.

CROSSROADS

Chapter Thirty-Eight

. . . .

"No!"

"Meaning?"

"I'm not talking about leaving Baltimore to continue service elsewhere. I'm talking about terminating active police work anywhere."

As per usual, Daddy was behind his desk, and I facing him. "And may I ask what's led to this conclusion?"

"Let me be forthright with you, sir. It has not addressed or fulfilled any of the reasons I entered police service."

"Son, you are still stressed out. I can hear it in your voice. Your decision to leave sounds premature and, frankly, poorly timed."

"My resignation goes beyond the purview of stress leave. It is purely a matter of conscience in a conscienceless occupation."

"And this, after almost ten years of service?"

"All I can say is I've tried, but I can't keep bullshitting myself any longer. I've come to believe that police work has become as demoralized and bankrupt as the people we inflict ourselves on."

"Has this anything to do with your relationship with . . . Marie?"

"Of course it does. It's just about wrecked that relationship to breaking point. I've made my choice. Recent events have proven my point, but it was a long time coming in my case."

"'Recent events'? Are you referring to Broadway's death?"

"I'm referring to my own experience in Broadway's pig pen—a reckless example of what surveillance work of that kind has come to, sir."

"Is that meant as a form of criticism?"

"Yes, sir. It is . . ."

"Well, we are being forthright, aren't we?" Daddy leaned back, worked his knuckles, and then rubbed them gently to soothe their long abuse. "In all this forthrightness, you neglected to tell me how you spent your . . . vacation time."

"Quietly. I rented a little house and didn't do much of anything."

"Except decide to give up your career. Anything else?"

"What are you after, sir?"

"November 12th was a very significant date as I recall, John. It was the day you promised . . ."

"The promise was kept. Frank Dixon's burn box was burned and the ashes scattered, as per our agreement, sir."

"So? And what about the knife?"

"The knife was tossed into the Harbor."

"Why the Harbor?"

"It's more final than burying it—and trying to hack a brand-new Kershaw to pieces is a dishonor to the object itself. I respect such things."

"Didn't you find it peculiar that both Dixon and Broadway met their deaths in the same manner? As unusual as it was a form of justice."

"Justice, yes. Peculiar, no."

"Why is that?," he asked, folding his hands.

"While I was in Pigtown, I discovered that, among Broadway's army of drug dealers and assassins, the art of the knife was legion."

"Is that so? The 'art of the knife'?"

"Yes, I know about such skills."

"That's right. Your training record indicates that you have great skills in the 'art of the knife.'"

"Yes, sir, and the use of hand weapons of various kinds. I was schooled in such and perhaps can make use of that knowledge in some other professional capacity. Or if not, abandon it entirely."

"Let's go back to your recent stress leave. We'll be here all night otherwise."

"What do you propose will end that tedious possibility, sir? I have a date to meet Marie for dinner, and I'm afraid further discussion can last only as long as the time I need to meet her."

"Another victory for forthrightness." Daddy rose from his chair and started pacing around the small room. He caught my puzzled expression. "I don't get enough exercise, John. I often pace the length of this office and the outside ones to make up for that lack. I can do it as many as three times a day."

"Is that what you're about to do, sir? Don't let me stand in your way." And I rose, as if to leave.

"No, I'm just reminding myself to do it after our talk."

"I don't know what there's left to say."

"One more question before you go . . ."

And I sat down, indicating my impatience.

"And that goes both ways."

"What does, sir?"

"You will answer a question of mine—forthrightly—and I, in turn, will answer a question of yours. Fair? How shall we do this?"

"It's your prerogative, sir."

"No, that would be taking advantage." And he put his hand inside his jacket pocket, fished around and brought out a quarter. He tossed it up in the air and caught it. He looked at me, as if he had done something spectacular. Suddenly, he put the quarter back in his jacket pocket.

"Son, I proposed this gambit. And, as your senior officer, I revoke it. I *will* take advantage of my position. That's what positions are all about, don't you agree?"

Again, I said nothing. He stood next to me. "Had you anything to do with Broadway's death?"

"No, sir," I lied forthrightly.

"Funny," he said, "I thought you had. I was going to offer my congratulations, in fact. If you hadn't, someone was bound to do it. Why not you?"

"There are enough assassins out to get Broadway as it is. Any one of them . . ."

"No, John, not anyone. It would have taken a special one. The Pigtown assholes were all in awe of him. Despite what they might have felt, none of them would have been capable."

"Besides," I followed up, "I never would have considered taking away any of the pleasurable prospects ahead for you, sir. Kill him for what?," and I flashed a winning smile.

"'Pleasurable prospects'?" he demanded.

"Well, your personal pleasure in seeing Broadway basted, roasted and generally skewered in a court of law."

"Yes, I admit there would have been some pleasure in nailing Broadway before his peers."

"Another form of killing—legit style. Wouldn't you agree, sir?"

"That's part of my job, Larkin—far outweighing any measure of personal 'pleasure' I might have derived from the proceeding."

216

"Well then, sir, you will have to wait for whoever replaces the kingpin to point the way to the killer."

"And we're back to that tiresome equation—again and again—are we?"

"You can't prevent that from happening . . . no matter what level of surveillance you throw around Pigtown. You know that, sir."

This stunning inevitability momentarily immobilized Daddy. He sat staring at me, not seeing me. It was my turn to question.

"What happened to Anthony Cerillo and Ralph Shaffer?"

"Who?" Daddy seemed genuinely lost.

"Maybe you'll remember their cover names—Anthony Alexander and Ralph Beane."

"Oh, yes, those boys. What about them?"

"They were undercover men in Pigtown in '06."

"You know, son, I don't really know. I lost contact with them. I do believe . . ."

"And did you lose contact with Frank?"

No answer. Stone face.

"Frank Dixon. Frank Keaton."

"Frank? Frank was losing track of himself. He was becoming Broadway's man."

"Are you sure of that?"

"He had become addicted."

"Is that why you gave up on him?"

"I just said—he gave up on himself. He had dishonored his mission, his assignment. God damn it, he was not the man I thought he was!"

"So, you gave up on him?"

"I've already answered your question. I'm only surprised Broadway didn't finish the job. He left it to us." And Daddy took his shades off, tossing them on his desk. He looked completely bewildered.

"We did the right thing by that boy. Besides, we gave him a first-class eulogy—thanks to you—and an officer's funeral, despite his . . . shortcomings."

"Would you have taken him back into S.I.S if he'd returned?"

"If . . . he had returned? I couldn't take that chance. In court, he would have had to admit to his addiction."

"And you wouldn't have defended him?"

"How could I have? And even if I had, who would have trusted such a man or his evidence?"

"Frank was relying on his trust in you to do the right thing and for all the other officers involved, when it came time, to speak out in court. Frank was a perfect example of what undercover officers are subjected to endure in the line of duty."

"Duty demands loyalty—and, in that, Dixon was remiss."

"Wasn't his coming back to S.I.S an indication of where his loyalty lay?"

"In Dixon's case, 'irresponsibility' is the better word for his actions." And suddenly Daddy let his anger go as never before. He rose and hovered over me.

"Larkin, by what stretch of your prodigious imagination do you think Dixon was coming back to S.I.S?"

"He was murdered outside Pigtown—he was returning home and had been followed, stabbed and then stripped of his identity."

"I don't need a history lesson from you, Larkin. Come to the point." His face was a mask of open hostility.

"OK, I myself read one of Frank's reports to you here at S.I.S, addressing that point—asking your pardon even. That was the real Frank Dixon speaking."

"How did you happen to see that report?"

"I was here when it came in. Yes, you want to fault me for it? Go ahead, sir. There would only be repercussions, sir, you know that. You never followed up on them. You left Frank dangling. Why? Why?"

"I already told you. He was junky."

"*Was*," I agreed. "Yes, probably. When in Rome, sir? But not when his body was found. Forensics reported no signs of drugs in his system, you know that! He was clean by then. He'd made himself clean!"

"Clean or not, he deserted his post. And by deserting it, Dixon put our entire team in jeopardy."

"Frank was an entirely separate cover. I doubt he had any awareness that there was another team working in Pigtown. I'm certain you made sure of that. It's part of S.I.S protocol, sir. It was only when Broadway gave his party and Fat Randy showed up that Frank took a walk, as we saw."

"Exactly—took a walk," Daddy hammered away.

"Frank was in no condition to do otherwise. His life was on the line. He had to walk."

"He walked, and our entire team disappeared from Pigtown with him."

"How do you mean that, sir?"

"The moment Frank Dixon deserted Broadway—for whatever reason—the jig was up. Whatever suspicions Broadway still had about Dixon were confirmed, and, obviously, Randy and Latrell became suspect. You can take it from there, Larkin."

"What's happened?" I asked lamely.

"While you were juggling with your 'conscience', the entire team disappeared, and Operation White Shadow's come to a standstill."

Suddenly showing great fatigue, Daddy fell back into his chair and put his shades back on.

"And J.B.?," I asked.

"J.B.—all the men—gone without a trace."

"What about Randy?"

"Randy, too. And he was right on the edge of getting what we needed—all those DC names." His fingers balled into a clenched fist, as if the DC freaks were in his grasp.

He stared out into space, as I wondered if he'd ever gotten those names, politically, what would he have done with them? Skewer them? Baste and burn them, too? Blackmail? Maybe, maybe not, or was Daddy seeking some foothold towards personal advantage? Meanwhile, I couldn't evade the image of all the "nicknames" being tossed into the Bay, their bloated bodies to surface come next spring's thaw.

"You took your chances, sir," I said quietly, "and it didn't work out as you'd planned it. I still feel that—if you'd supported Frank in the coming trials—he would have been your star witness in nailing Broadway. And that was the main objective, wasn't it?"

Daddy looked at me with a slight sneer on his face.

"Larkin, I've had you all wrong. You are a boy scout, after all. Like most people, the DC boys look out for their own interests. The country comes second. The loaded guns are mostly in the hands of the diehards and closet bigots and a small, but wealthy set of freaks who like to attend Broadway's parties. The uprights form a small minority. The games the majority play to get what they want is the precise definition of the word 'politics'. I know those games—I've seen them recycled in my lifetime time and time again. I could show those motherfuckers a thing or two. They would have rallied behind

Broadway, if only to get invited back to those parties. Dixon would have been eaten alive. Get the picture? History lesson over! Class dismissed!" And, with a sharp lift of his chin, "I don't want you to be late for your appointment."

"What do you want?," I asked suspiciously.

"I want a personal letter of resignation from you, and I want it by tomorrow. If I'm not here, you can leave it with Jennifer. She'll be handling such matters until I've re-staffed. You can clear your and Dixon's lockers of whatever is in there. Meanwhile, you need to turn in your badge and gun."

I stood—silent—not quite believing my long ordeal was actually over. Daddy's voice began to harden.

"Incidentally," he said, "I don't believe you about Broadway. Personally, I think you did it, YOU-SON-OF-A-BITCH!" he shouted.

I looked at him and said quietly, "I'm not your son, Gailbrait."

I had never seen such a look of astonishment on Daddy's face before. Without looking at him now, I removed the badge clipped to my belt, lifted my right foot on to the chair I'd occupied, raised my trouser leg and released the Glock from my ankle. I placed the badge and pistol on his desk. My hand lingered on the weapon. In a personal farewell, I touched its trigger, holding it in place for a few seconds. As I did so, I could sense Daddy flinching in his chair. I waited—then turned the gun's handle around towards him and pushed it and the badge slowly forward.

Without another word, I left his office leaving Gailbrait Smith, AKA Daddy, staring at my shorn equipment of police entitlement.

I'd already decided not to render in my resignation by hand, but rather to wire it in as my final report to S.I.S. As the pigeon shit hit my nostrils, I knew it was for the last time. Feeling like a convict just released from prison, I jumped into my SUV and eased it out of the warehouse, leaving behind me the image of the avenging angel in dark shades, slumped in his chair.

I didn't look back.

Chapter Thirty-Nine

I was already at the restaurant. Everything was on tap awaiting Marie's arrival. She was due back late this afternoon. Meeting her at the apartment would have spoiled my preparations, and her surprise. She was due to arrive at 7:30. The table was already set. No flowers to obscure our view of one another. Just a single red rose on a small piece of chinaware holding a smaller velvet box. The menu had been decided on and a bottle of Prosecco was already cooling in a silver beaker by the side of the table. My watch registered 7:40 when I checked it. At 7:45, I was about to try her again on her cell. It rang, but I could hear it ringing close by. I looked up, and there she was, sitting in the chair opposite me—and I hung up the phone.

"The train was an hour late," she said a little out of breath. "I didn't have time to stop at the apartment, so I came right over to meet you. My bag is outside in checking," and then we just stared at one another. Marie looked more beautiful than ever—more composed even—dressed in a twill jacket with a finely pleated skirt. There were pearls around her neck, and a small pair of matching earrings.

"Did you change on the train?," I asked. "I mean you look so right, for right now."

"No, I just came as I was dressed. I took a local at Groton and changed at New Haven. That's where all the mix-up was. I called but got no answer—and here I am only fifteen minutes late."

"What were you doing in Groton? I thought Alicia lived in Milton."

"She does," Marie nodded her head. "I left her early this morning to do what I had to do. What's this?" She was looking at the china dish, then looked at me, blushed and swallowed hard.

"Well, go on," I said. "Open it," and I leaned back in my chair, knowing I was looking as appropriately smart as she, in my Larkin & Associates pearl grey suit. Marie's fingers rose to hover over the box, then they lowered slowly to open it. A little shiver went through her. She kept her eyes downcast looking at her new diamond engagement ring. When she looked at me again, tears were beginning to well up, and she shut the box with a quick, light touch.

"You don't like it?" I was abashed at that possibility. "It's 1.5 karats."

She shook her head repeatedly, which I took as a confirmation of my statement.

Marie, realizing that, said, "No, Johnny. It's not that. It's not that at all. It's . . . extraordinary," and she very quickly picked up the napkin to daub at her eyes. She then looked around her and blessedly it was a slow night with only a few customers at a good distance from our table. Marie then looked at the champagne bottle cooling in the silver beaker.

"It's not domestic, I can assure you," I said with a self satisfied grin. A waiter suddenly appeared from nowhere, ready to move into action.

"Vintage Prosecco Di Conegliano," he repeated the wine's name. "We call it the Soave Fan Ciulla of champagne."

"That's Italian," Marie said, "Am I right?" The waiter beamed his assent.

"What does it mean?," she asked.

"To translate it properly would be a little difficult."

"Well, roughly, then. What does it mean?"

"Smooth—a most delightful young lady," he managed, "And many other delectable things."

"Say it to me," she asked and he did.

"Sounds like something from an opera."

"It is. By Puccini, from La Boheme."

"I know those names," Marie said a little proudly.

"May I oblige then, Signori?," the waiter cajoled.

"No, not just yet—thank you."

"You may only look in my direction," and he pointed at his spot, "When you are ready," and with a slight bow in both our directions, he moved quietly back to his 'spot'.

Marie looked back to me. "He was flirting with me," she said in a hushed voice.

"Well, does it surprise you? Just look at you."

"I won't taste a drop of that Soave Fan Ciulla," pronouncing it quite adequately, "until I've had my say. Incidentally, that's a new suit. I've never seen you in grey. You look smashing. No blue, what a relief. It's just that I need to answer your questions," she said quite frankly.

"Which?"

"Why I was taking the local at Groton. It's just that I did what I needed to do for a long time. I went up there."

"What's in Groton?"

"Grace Hobart lives there."

"And who is Grace Hobart?"

"My mother. My birth mother."

"No," and I leaned back to hear the rest.

"I finally forced Alicia to give me the information she had withheld from me for all these years. She was desolate at the thought of possibly losing me, of my being disappointed—shocked even. I assured that her I would never leave her and that she would always be my mother. Look at what she'd done—practically bringing me up by herself. A widow after my father died. She wept, and I consoled her. I've never forgotten what she's done for me. Just that now I'm hoping to get married—I needed to know. She reluctantly gave it to me—admitting she had withheld it this long, for my sake. After all, who would give up a child if it didn't signify some desperate need to do so? I haven't told her anything yet at what happened. But of course I will. I wanted you to be the first to know. So I rented a car and drove up to Groton, a mill town. I had Grace Hobart's telephone number but not her address, and she answered when I called. She sounded rather cool and all together when I told her who I was, and when I asked if I could see her, she gave me instructions to meet her at a tea place somewhere in town 'before I do my marketing', she said. I got to the tea place first, and she arrived ten minutes later, driving a cozy looking Impala. She was casually dressed in her country jeans and matching shirt with a light wrap around her shoulders. She wore new white sneakers and a saucy engineer's cap over her 'mod' hairdo. She is a pretty, little woman and I felt like an idiot dressed to the nines for our 'reconciliation'. First thing I noticed were her cheek bones. Here they are," and she touched her own lightly.

"Grace Hobart is in her mid-fifties. I didn't know what to do—embrace her, kiss her cheeks or what. As she approached me, she offered her solution. She put out her hand, so we shook hands. I noticed they were carefully manicured. Despite the cute engineer's cap, everything about her was carefully coiffed and lacquered. We sized one another as we sipped herbal tea and munched on some oatmeal cookies. She was as cool as a cucumber and spoke in some high-toned speech pattern, and I sat eating her up. Here she was—my biological mother. The sum of it was that Grace had had a fling with a college student back in Villanova, PA. And the result was sitting there ogling her. Marie, the name she had written on the card pinned to my blanket, she considered a generic name that would suit whoever or whatever I would turn out to be in future. She and my birth father broke up immediately after—promising to keep in touch, which they managed for a bit. We sat for an hour until she remembered she had marketing to do for the family. The Hobarts consisted of one very well-to-do husband in real estate, herself, and two pre-college girls. When I asked if I could meet them, the cheekbones tightened and she let it slip." Marie paused again, I think a little overwhelmed by what followed. She drank some water before going on.

"Not on your life,' she said. 'Miss Racaud. Not on your life. They know nothing of your existence, and I intend to keep things that way.'

"I was tempted to dump my tea tray into her lap. I didn't, but I wish I had now, the bitch! I asked about my father. Recovering her cool and without any hesitation she wrote down his name and a number I might reach him at.

"She then stood up and said, 'Well, thank God you turned out attractive,' and out came the hand. I looked at it but didn't take it.

"'I understand,' she said. 'I'd probably have done the same thing if I were in your shoes.' "And she drove off in the Impala to do her marketing."

"And did you call him?," I asked in the brief silence that followed.

"Of course I did, as soon as she had gone. His name is Richard Quenelle, and he has a professorship post at Dartmouth. He certainly sounded a little dry, making him seem much older than he might be.

"'Well, Miss Racaud,' he said when I reached him. 'I'm happy to know you are alive and well. But as for seeing you I don't think that is a sound idea.'

"'I've been thinking about you for years, wondering about you, and now, speaking to you . . .'"

"'I understand,' he said, 'But then what else is there to say? It was at one of these fraternity parties—too much to drink—and a stranger was born as a result. And a stranger you have remained and will always remain, my dear Miss Picauld, is it?'

"'Ricaut,' I shouted, and I continued to plead with him to give me a chance. That's when he got tough!

"'Look Miss, whatever your name is. My advice is to let things remain what they are. Who gave you this number in the first place?'

"I told him.

"'Goddam that bitch! After all these years she's still blaming me for what was her fault.' And suddenly I said, 'I'm getting married.'

"'Congratulations,' he replied courteously.

"'I thought you'd like to know and even consider coming to . . .'

"'Look,' he said, 'I hope you have a happy life but this conversation has come to an end.'

"'No, Mr. Quenelle . . . please.'

"'I suggest you not try contacting me again,' and he hung up . . . and that's how I came to be taking the local at Groton. When you caught me on the cell, I was in New Haven waiting for the train. I can't tell you how I felt hearing a friendly voice—and especially yours."

She closed her eyes for a whole minute putting all she'd experienced in order. When she opened them she took the ring box and flicked it open. She held the ring in the palm of her hand. I immediately got up and went to kneel by her side. I took the ring and slipped it on to her finger.

She looked at the ring then at me and said, "Johnny, John, let's have lots and lots of children so our calendar will be filled with baptisms and engagements. We'll get to know all those aunties of mine out there, and their children will really get to know me—and us—instead of being cards at Christmas from people I wouldn't know if I met them. And we must make sure our families, your mother and father and all theirs will never lose sight of each other—and us—whatever happens. I love you, Johnny, as much as you love me. Can you imagine how much that is?"

And Marie rose up out of her chair and I with her. It was the most violently tender clinch we have ever managed. And the kiss!

For a bonus, she kissed me on the forehead—my favorite spot. There was a loud applause and some cheering. The restaurant was now full, and all eyes were on us. We stood there holding hands, and you know what? The waiter told us the entire evening was on the house—courtesy of the management. As the waiter poured the Soave Fan Cuilla, I could hear Frank's voice, "We've made it." Then he winked.

Chapter Forty

The next morning, Marie wanted to visit some friends at the hospital. Before we had breakfast, she watched as I hauled out from the closets all my officer's clothes and paraphernalia—shoes, socks, shirts, hats—everything including stray badges, holsters, things I found tucked away in unexpected places. Most of the citations and stray paperwork I consigned to a large carton. Marie helped me pile the stuff in the back of our rented car. She waited in the parking area of the police headquarters' downtown building where, with the help of a rookie, I deposited all the stuff on the table of the Quartermaster's office in the building's basement—as per the rules. I then drove Marie to the hospital. Marie's own resignation had spurred me on to my decision. Whether I would ever divulge any of my Broadway story was doubtful. I had accomplished what I needed to do for Frank and myself and, in that bargain, for Marie. It would remain my one lingering secret. She watched me as the clothes, etc., disappeared from the car—relishing the tangible evidence of my decision. It was over. Frank and I had undertaken the summons of our calling to help save the world. We had entered the jungle of Baltimore City armed mostly with our righteousness on its behalf. In the process, we became the very beasts we had come to tame. I'd been left to live to become human again. I hoped the same for all the inhabitants of Pigtown.

I went back to the apartment and wrote my letter of resignation to S.I.S. I then dialed a long distance number to my alma mater in Boston—I'd left over a decade before. The voice of my mentor came as a welcome shock. Professor Adam Celestini, whose name I had chosen for my cover in Pigtown, was alive and well—at sixty-eight, still head of his division of the Criminal Justice Department at Northeastern University. As we spoke, it could have been the day after I'd said goodbye to him following graduation. For an hour, we caught up. Adam Celestini, in his own career, had been 'out there'. He'd been caught in the revolving door of the laws of inefficiency and degradation. Had confronted chaos and survived. Why wouldn't I? But there were other matters to discuss—equally as important. We made an appointment for lunch the following week at our favorite Boston pub. It would be like old times.

FATE
AND
CHANCE

Chapter Forty-One

Thanksgiving holidays were approaching, and an invitation by my parents for Marie and me to join them in Old Saybrook seemed an opportune way to celebrate my leaving the police force—and a chance for my parents to become better acquainted with their future daughter-in-law. Naturally there would be more talk about Larkin Associates.

Through the internet, Marie had relocated herself to a hospital in Cambridge, Massachusetts, commencing after the New Year. A daytime shift had been Marie's only prerequisite.

My continuing conversations with Adam Celestini opened up the possibility of my entering into a contract—professorship available to former students—for one year, to go into effect in the fall of '09. A possibility with a catch to it—namely the necessity to find a new coach for the crew team, to be inaugurated this coming March. I leapt at that idea. Crew, besides hunting, had been my sport while studying at Northeastern. I saw this as a bonus, happy to again be working the waters of the Charles River. I would need to have no fear of a body bobbing up between oar strokes. The goddess Serendipity was being generous with her holiday gifts. Most importantly, I needed to communicate the dangers now facing the new group of Criminal Justice graduates.

Based on our mutual good luck, Marie and I decided to relocate our "collectibles" to Cambridge, where we found a small apartment available in a hotel—apartment complex near Cambridge University until we could settle on more permanent digs.

After spending the Christmas holidays with Alicia, we still had a few days left in Baltimore to clean our slate.

If all this and what follows seems like so much tidying up, there is nothing pejorative about that. In an untidy world—when tidying up is needed—there's nothing more reassuring and life-affirming. Particularly, if it concerns people in our lives, tidying up means that, in some way, we cared about having met and been friends, even for a while.

After closing our bank accounts, I went up to Hogan's Alley with a particular intention besides hellos. It was to use Frank's legacy money to pay up his severely delinquent tab. Hogan would have none of it. He refused even to tabulate the monies due. "That way, Frank would still be with us." Hogan then led me over to our old booth and pointed up to the wall enclosing it. There was a new addition to the gallery—a picture of Frank and myself, in uniform, taken at our indoctrination at the Academy. How young we looked. And how incredibly hopeful for what was up ahead.

When I insisted again on paying Frank's debt, Hogan countered with, "Send the money, in my name, to the Fund for Handicapped Iraqi Veterans. I think Frank would approve of that move." There were tears in his eyes as we hugged our goodbyes, with promises to write, "if only at Christmas." I promised I would.

The next day, Marie and I went to the Delaney Valley Memorial Cemetery to pay a last visit to Frank's grave. Would we ever come this way again? Fate and chance would take care of that. Meanwhile, we'd made provisions for Frank's grave to be attended and cared for. I'd called the Rochester cemetery where Frank's parents and sister, Bea, were buried—the unpronounceable M on the tombstone was "Müybåckýte". As a former officer at S.I.S, I had prevailed on the cutter to eliminate "Dixon" and put the old family name in its place. It was accomplished at medium cost and maximum understanding on the part of the cutter, who stood by us as the finished stone was put in its proper place. I traced the letters with my fingers. The cutter's pride at accommodating and fitting in the new name was evident as I shook his hand to congratulate the man for his work.

Marie knelt and placed some flowers under the unpronounceable and quietly sounded the foreign name as best she could. It was a kind of baptismal rite of sorts, and we both felt it to be a fitting end to it all. I leaned down, picked up some dirt from Frank's grave and put it in an envelope which contained the rosary. I sealed the envelope and put it in the inside pocket of my jacket.

All of a sudden, it started to snow . . . softly . . . real snow.

The End